DEAD EASY
FOR DOVER

DEAD EASY
FOR DOVER

Joyce Porter

A Foul Play Press Book

The Countryman Press, Inc.
Woodstock, Vermont

To
Mary and Harry Brazier,
with much affection

Copyright © 1978 by Joyce Porter

This edition first published in 1991 by Foul Play Press,
an imprint of The Countryman Press, Inc.,
Woodstock, Vermont 05091

ISBN 0-88150-212-X

Printed in the United States of America

10 9 8 7 6 5 4 3 2 1

I

The inhabitants of Frenchy Botham were not best pleased one blustery March morning to find that they had got a murder on their hands. The few remaining 'real' villagers (those with the peeling paint and the front gardens full of rotting cabbages) didn't want packs of bloody bobbies poking about for any reason whatsoever, while the townees hadn't spent all that money on their country retreats just to have dead bodies dumped in their well-kept shrubberies.

The Chief Constable gazed despondently at the tarpaulin-covered bundle at his feet and slapped his swagger stick anxiously into a leather-gloved palm. 'Are you sure there's no identification on the body?' he asked for the fifth time.

Detective Inspector Walters was a big man with a matching supply of patience. He stuck placidly to the formula which had served him well on four previous occasions. 'Nothing we've been able to find so far, sir,' he said. 'Mind you, we haven't been able to strip her yet, but there's nothing in the pockets and there's no sign of a handbag.'

'But you're still looking?'

'For the handbag, sir?' Inspector Walters indicated a posse of policemen who were meticulously examining every square inch of the garden, the drive and the roadway outside. 'Yes, we're still looking.'

The Chief Constable gnawed industriously at his bottom lip. 'Damn and blast!' he said.

'You'll be calling in Scotland Yard, sir?' The Inspector already knew the answer and accepted the implied slur on his capabilities with admirable resignation.

'I rang London before I came out here,' muttered the Chief Constable, a man who avoided responsibility like other people avoid the plague. 'They should be here in a couple of hours.'

'Oh, well, we can't move the body till they've seen it, I suppose,' observed Inspector Walters, talking as much to save embarrassing pauses as for any other reason. 'I've already commandeered the Memorial Hall for use as a Serious Incidents Room. It'll all be properly fitted up and staffed by the time the Murder Squad chaps get down here.'

'If she'd been a local girl,' said the Chief Constable miserably, 'I wouldn't have hesitated for a moment. We'd have tackled it ourselves. But she isn't.'

'Apparently not, sir,' agreed Inspector Walters stolidly.

'It's well on the cards that Frenchy Botham's connection with this murder is purely accidental. The girl was probably just dumped here from a passing car or something and there'll be ramifications stretching way beyond our area of jurisdiction. It's got all the hallmarks of being the sort of case that Scotland Yard can cope with standing on its head.'

'Quite so, sir.'

Inspector Walters's tone was soothing but the Chief Constable was still in the grip of an overwhelming need to justify himself. 'We just don't have the facilities,' he pointed out. 'Nor the experience. Nor the man-power. This flu epidemic has really hit us, you know. I see our overall strength figures every morning and, believe me, they're frightening. Quite frightening.' He lashed out at a nearby rhododendron bush with his swagger stick and sought for a change of conversation. 'How long did you say she'd been lying here?'

Inspector Walters shook his head. 'I didn't, sir. But, going by the state of her clothing, it'll be days rather than hours. Doctor Maxton thought it could be weeks, but that was after only a superficial examination. We'll have a bit more of an idea, perhaps, after the P.M.'

'Had she been . . ?'

'Didn't look like it, sir. The clothing isn't torn or even disarranged, come to that. And those jeans she was wearing are so blooming tight I reckon you'd need a tin opener to get her out of them, if you follow me.'

It was starting to rain again. The Chief Constable turned up his coat collar and asked another question. He was anxious not to appear to be beating too hasty a retreat back to the warmth and dryness of his office while the men under his command were obliged to continue with their search, however inclement the weather.

Inspector Walters shook his head again. 'No, she wasn't strangled, sir, and I suppose you could take that as another slight indication that we're not dealing with a case of rape or sexual assault. As a matter of fact, she seems to have been struck across the back of the head with the proverbial blunt instrument. The skull's crushed, apparently. The doctor reckons there would be very little bleeding. He's got half an idea that she was still alive when she was dumped here, but he's only guessing at the moment.'

'She definitely wasn't killed where she was found?'

'Seems not, sir.'

The Chief Constable could feel the rain trickling down the back of his neck but he carried on bravely. 'It seems an odd sort of place to have hidden her.'

'Oh, I don't know, sir.' Inspector Walters surveyed the terrain thoughtfully. 'I've noticed these biggish detached houses with their own bits of driveways before. They nearly always leave the gates wide open. Too much trouble to keep nipping in and out of their cars, otherwise. To say nothing of tradesmen and such like.'

The Chief Constable shifted his weight from one sodden foot to the other. 'What about keeping children in – or dogs?'

'Usually confined to the back gardens, in my experience, sir. Besides, you can see for yourself.' Inspector Walters began moving in the direction of the Chief Constable's car, and gesticulated along the road. 'Every house here in The Grove has got its drive gates pushed more or less permanently open. To say nothing of the fact that they don't have any kids or pet animals here at Les Chênes.'

The Chief Constable was a mite over-sensitive. 'You're not trying to suggest that the murderer had local knowledge, are you, Walters?'

'Not really sir,' came the imperturbable rejoinder. 'Though I think it'd be a mistake to rule out a local villain entirely. With reasonable luck, you know, that body could have lain there out of sight behind the open gate for months. It was virtually hidden by those bushes.

'Oh, I don't think we can use that sort of speculation as the basis for anything, old chap.' The Chief Constable was growing bolder as he found his car almost within touching distance. 'It's only a few feet away from a public thoroughfare, for heaven's sake! And what about gardening?'

Inspector Walters had his own theories and was massively unmoved. 'You'd be surprised, sir,' he said, 'how very few people walk along The Grove on foot. Or peer over quite a high stone wall when they do. And there isn't, sir,' he pointed out heavily, 'all that much in the way of gardening to be done under a clump of overgrown rhododendron bushes.'

The Chief Constable was determined not to have this labelled a local crime if he could help it. 'But the body *was* discovered!' he insisted with ill-concealed triumph. 'That proves it can't have been hidden away as cleverly as all that, doesn't it?'

'It was only discovered because old Sir Perceval Henty-Harris died, sir.'

The Chief Constable scowled at his driver who was displaying a marked reluctance to get out of the car and open the door. 'What do you mean, it was only because old Sir Perceval died?'

'If he hadn't finally kicked the bucket, sir, his niece wouldn't have been going off for a bit of a holiday, would she, sir? That's why she closed the gates. She said she thought it made the house look less unoccupied, and she's scared stiff of burglars breaking in at the best of times.'

The police driver had finally emerged and was standing resentfully out in the rain with the door open. The Chief Constable determined to teach him a lesson. 'So it was Miss Henty-Harris who discovered the body?'

Inspector Walters had himself briefed the Chief Constable on this particular point, but he scorned to show even a flicker of surprise at the question. 'That's right, sir. She decided to postpone her holiday and phoned us.'

The Chief Constable nodded his approval at this piece of co-operation on the part of the general public and decided that his driver had now suffered enough. 'Oh, well, back to the paperwork, I suppose!' he lamented unconvincingly. 'You've no idea how much I envy you chaps out in the field.' He got into his shiny black official car and pressed the switch which lowered the window. 'I can leave you to look after these people from the Murder Squad, can I, Walters? Every courtesy and consideration, you know. Total support. Well, we're all on the same side, aren't we?'

Detective Inspector Walters inclined his head. 'So they tell me, sir.' He got a last question in as the driver revved his engine impatiently. 'Who are they sending us, sir? Have you any idea?'

'A chappie called Dover,' said the Chief Constable, spreading himself happily over the real leather. 'One of these young, up-and-coming, high-flying types, I imagine.'

'What makes you think that, sir?'

'Well, he's only a chief inspector and he's supernumerary – so the Commander was telling me. Obviously some bright young spark they're anxious to hang on to till he's ready for promotion and they've got a vacancy. I reckon we've drawn a real whizz kid.' Something in Inspector Walters's face gave the Chief Constable pause. 'You don't know him, do you?'

'I must be thinking of somebody else, sir.'

'Oh, well, bring him over to see me as soon as you've got him settled in.' The Chief Constable flapped an imperious hand. 'Drive on, Harvey!'

A*

Inspector Walters sighed. The only Detective Chief Inspector Dover he'd ever heard of up at the Yard was old Wilfred – and whizz kid he was not. On the contrary, he was a middle-aged down-and-out who, if rumour was to be believed, had only got within a hundred miles of the élite Murder Squad because nobody else in the rest of the Metropolitan Police would have him. And, far from awaiting further promotion, it was generally accepted that he'd reached his professional ceiling years ago as probationary constable.

Inspector Walters watched the Chief Constable's car disappear down the road. Oh, well, it was probably all a bit exaggerated. Old Wilfred couldn't be as bad as all that or he'd have been booted out years ago. Surely? Of course, they did say if there was one thing the old fool was an expert at it was saving his own skin. And then his sergeant was reputed to be pretty much on the ball, and that probably enhanced Dover's powers of survival. Inspector Walters frowned. Now, what was the lad's name? A handsome young buck, by all accounts, and something of a snappy dresser. Supposed to write a letter once a week to the Commissioner begging for a transfer. It didn't matter where to – dog handling or traffic or the bomb squad – just as long as it was away from Wilfred Dover. Inspector Walters searched his memory. Ah, MacGregor! That was it. Sergeant MacGregor. Poor devil!

Inspector Walters contemplated what lay before him during the next few days and sighed again. Oh, well, he reminded himself with typical lack of originality, a policeman's lot was not a happy one and the only way to deal with life's little problems is to grin and bear them. He squared his shoulders and, turning away, marched off to see how his men were getting on with their search.

As it so happens, Inspector Walters had been doing Detective Chief Inspector Dover a gross injustice. True – the old Dover had indeed been a fat, lazy, unhealthy, unintelligent and none-too-honest slob of the first magnitude, but all that had now changed.

Dover himself, his filthy boots resting disgustingly on the opposite seat, explained the metamorphosis to his sergeant as they journeyed down in the train to the scene of this latest murder. The explanation was necessary because, to Sergeant MacGregor's jaundiced eye at least, outward appearances seemed much the same as usual. The little black eyes appeared as malevolent as ever, the face as podgy and the complexion as pasty. That dreadful overcoat with its dandruff-encrusted shoulders was stretched as tightly as before over the swelling paunch and that greasy bowler hat was still brooding as squalidly over its owner's ignoble brow – a long way over, actually, as Dover had reverentially deposited it on the rack for the duration of the trip.

No, MacGregor could see no evidence of any physical change whatsoever.

'Commerce,' explained Dover when he'd managed to extricate a bit of his pie crust from behind his upper set. 'Trade. Industry. Big business. That's where it's all happening. A seat on the board of directors and' – his eyes grew quite misty at the prospect – 'unlimited expenses.'

MacGregor had had his hopes blasted too often in the past to start counting chickens now. Still, the question had to be asked. 'Are you thinking of – er – leaving the police, sir?'

'Got beyond the thinking stage, laddie!' boasted Dover whose bows were rarely drawn on the short side. 'Virtually all over bar the shouting.'

'Really, sir?'

Just in case British Rail's carriages had ears, Dover edged closer to the shrinking MacGregor and lowered his voice. 'Haven't told Them yet, of course,' he grunted. 'Why the hell should I? 'Strewth, I don't owe Them anything. And to hell with the pension!' He paused before adding somewhat illogically, 'Besides, I don't want to give Them the opportunity of talking me out of it.'

MacGregor was an articulate young man who had been educated at one of our minor Public Schools. He was not often at a loss for words. Nor was he on this occasion. 'Oh, quite, sir,' he said from a very dry throat.

'Pomeroy Chemicals Limited,' said Dover, expelling the magic formula in a spray of soggy pie crust. 'Chief Security Officer. Salary subject to negotiation so the sky's the limit, eh? Here' – he tossed the packet of cheese and pickle sandwiches into Mac-Gregor's more capable hands – 'get this bloody thing open for me!'

MacGregor forced his way through the plastic. 'And you've actually got this job, sir?'

'Got the application form,' said Dover, stuffing an entire cheese and pickle sandwich into his mouth so as to leave his hands free for grubbing through his pockets. 'Don't reckon I'll have much to fear in the way of competition.' He chuckled complacently. 'There won't be many applicants with a record like mine!'

MacGregor thought that this was probably true and waited with interest while Dover first found and then flattened out with fingers still greasy from the cheese sandwich a dog-eared and ruinous wad of paper.

'It's this bit I want to talk to you about,' said Dover, handing over one of the sheets.

MacGregor accepted it, grateful that he'd kept his gloves on against the cold.

'That bit there,' said Dover. 'Where it says: *List what you consider are the highlights of your professional career (with dates).*'

MacGregor could appreciate that this section might indeed cause difficulty.

'What you've got to remember,' said Dover, reaching for another cheese sandwich, 'is that these people aren't interested in the past. Last week's ancient history to them. It's what's happening here and now that impresses them. That's why I want to go out on a winning streak.'

'You mean this case we're going to investigate at Frenchy Botham, sir.'

'Precisely!' Dover regarded MacGregor with an almost benevolent eye and made a mental note to try and work it in somewhere in that questionnaire that he was something of a wizard when it came to selecting and training bright young men. 'I want a really spectacular success, and I want it fast. With the maximum publicity, of course. My past record can naturally stand on its own feet but it's my handling of this case that's going to count with those Pomeroy Chemical boys.' Dover glanced suspiciously at his sergeant. 'I hope I can rely on your co-operation.'

MacGregor was a reticent person. Otherwise he might have been tempted to assure Dover that, to get him that plum job at Pomeroy Chemicals, he (MacGregor) would willingly face any dangers, brave any hazards (up to and including walking on red-hot coals), work any hours and solve any problems. In short, Sergeant MacGregor could place his hand on his heart and proclaim with all sincerity that there was nothing he wouldn't do to get rid of Dover.

But Dover wasn't even listening to the much more muted declaration of loyalty which MacGregor eventually produced. He was looking for his cheese and pickle sandwiches.

'But you've eaten them all, sir!'

Dover's National Health dentures bared in an ugly snarl. 'Rubbish!'

'You did, honestly, sir!'

'Well, in that case, laddie,' said Dover, leaning back and folding his arms, 'you'd better get me some more, hadn't you? You can't expect me to work at top pressure on a bloody empty stomach. And fetch me a piece of cake while you're at it!'

But the time always comes when the eating has to stop and eventually Dover and MacGregor arrived in Frenchy Botham. They were welcomed by an impassive Inspector Walters who explained he had given orders that nothing be moved until their arrival and, under his guidance, they duly inspected the body which was still lying where it had been found. They made a cursory inspection of the surroundings and listened to a succinct account from Inspector Walters of the progress so far. All in all a good five minutes was spent at the scene of the crime before Dover's patience and his feet gave out at pretty much the same time.

''Strewth, it's a bit nippy out here!' said Dover, breaking into Inspector Walters's dissertation on the murder's apparent lack of sexual connotations.

Inspector Walters just wasn't quick enough. Before he had time to switch his mind to this new topic of conversation, he found he'd lost his audience. Dover was already three-quarters of the way back to the waiting police car and Sergeant Mac-Gregor was hot-footing it after him. Inspector Walters paused only to tell the ambulance men that the body could now be removed before joining in the chase. He caught up with his main quarry just as it was depositing seventeen and a quarter stone of unlovely fat with a deep sigh of relief on the back seat of the car.

'We've established the Murder Headquarters in the Village Hall, sir,' panted Inspector Walters, naïvely confident that this information would be of interest.

Dover's lip curled and his little black moustache (of the style made so unpopular by Adolf Hitler forty years ago) twitched contemptuously. He had yet to meet either a Murder Headquarters or a village hall which came anywhere near his standards of comfort. 'Stuff that for a lark! I'll be directing operations from this room you're supposed to have booked for me.'

'At The Laughing Dog, sir?' Inspector Walters was already beginning to crack.

Luckily his foolish question provided Dover with an early opportunity to display the rapier-like wit for which he was so well known. 'Unless you've managed to get me a bed at Buckingham Palace!'

'But . . .'

Dover ceased sniggering at his own cleverness and spelt it out. 'I'm going back to my room in this boozer place to have a quiet think,' he said, slowly and clearly. 'And I don't want to be disturbed.' He noticed that Inspector Walters was opening and closing his mouth like a drowning goldfish and graciously condescended to explain his methods a little more fully. 'It's brains that make a great detective, laddie,' he announced, solemnly tapping the side of his forehead with a grubby finger. 'You don't find real experts like me rushing around like a scalded cat on hot bricks. Take it from me, laddie – my " quiet thinks " have solved more murders than you've had hot bloody dinners.'

MacGregor, who was installed next to Dover on the back seat, stared unblinkingly straight ahead.

But Inspector Walters still hovered. 'Er – what do you want me to do then, sir?'

'How about just buggering off, eh?' demanded Dover, discarding his philosophical role somewhat abruptly.

'But what about Mr Plum, sir?'

'Mr Plum? Who the hell's Mr Plum when he's at home?'

'He's the landlord of The Laughing Dog, sir. That's the village pub you and Sergeant MacGregor will be staying in. Mr Plum apparently has some information about the girl.'

Dover frowned. 'What girl?'

'The dead one, sir.' Inspector Walters glanced at MacGregor but there was no help coming from that quarter. 'I've had all my chaps out making house-to-house enquiries round the village, and this is the only lead they've come up with.'

Dover thought of Pomeroy Chemicals Limited. 'Oh, all right,' he growled irritably, 'let's be having it!'

Inspector Walters was embarrassed. 'Well, that's the trouble, sir. He wouldn't tell us. Not my constable, that is. He said he'd got some important information about the girl and he was blowed if he was going to divulge it to some baby-faced copper who wasn't dry behind the ears yet. My constable attempted to remonstrate with him, of course, but Mr Plum was adamant. It was Scotland Yard or nothing, he said.'

All things considered, Dover took the news surprisingly well. Usually the very idea of work was anathema to him, but he reflected that landlords of public houses are not as other men. And, who knows? A little friendly interview at this stage in the game might well develop into a truly lasting and profitable association. 'All right,' he said. 'I'll see to What's-his-name. Meantime, you just carry on!'

Inspector Walters tried to hold the car back by brute force. 'But, sir,' he bleated, having failed to achieve his initial object and now being forced to run alongside with his head stuck through the open window, 'the Chief Constable . . .'

'Oh, stuff the Chief Constable!' retorted Dover and, unexpectedly bestirring himself, attempted to wind up the window fast enough to trap Inspector Walters by the throat. He missed by no more than the tip of a nose. 'We're going to have to watch that joker,' he gasped as he sank back exhausted in his seat.

'I thought he seemed quite a decent sort of chap, sir.'

Dover regarded MacGregor sourly. 'Did you? Well, just see you keep him out of my hair, that's all. I don't want him messing things up.'

'Very good, sir.'

'And I don't want you messing things up, either!' added Dover viciously. 'This is my bloody case and I'm going to solve it in my own bloody way. Savee?'

These days MacGregor didn't even permit himself the luxury of irony in his thoughts. 'Yes, sir,' he said meekly. 'I understand perfectly.'

2

Both Mr Plum, landlord of The Laughing Dog, and Dover were in the habit of taking a nap in the afternoon (though in deference to his new and dynamic persona, Dover this time kept his boots on when he stretched out on the eiderdown), so it was getting on for five o'clock before their encounter took place. Mr Plum, much refreshed, presented himself in Dover's bedroom with a loaded tea tray and thus acquired the great detective's instant and whole-hearted attention.

MacGregor, armed with a notebook and a newly sharpened pencil, resigned himself to conducting the interview and duly raised his voice to cover the sounds of Dover's uninhibited mastication. 'I understand, Mr Plum, that you've got some information for us about this young woman who's been found dead?'

Mr Plum, a well-padded man with whiskers that looked as though they'd been tended by a topiarian, settled himself more securely in the other easy chair. He was there to enjoy himself and had no intention of being hurried. 'That's right, sergeant,' he agreed easily. 'And, going by what I've heard about this murder, I reckon my evidence is going to be vital. That's why I decided to save it for Scotland Yard. I'm sure our local policemen are wonderful when it comes to motoring offences and enforcing the licensing laws, but – murder? No, I fancy they might find themselves a touch out of their depth there.'

Dover, being post a sardine sandwich and ante a cream horn, was free to ask a question. 'Where,' he demanded indignantly, 'is the bloody sugar?'

'Under the plate of scones, squire!' Mr Plum leaned across to assist. 'See?'

MacGregor knew – none better – to what unspeakable depths these interviews could sink if Dover was allowed to keep interrupting, and he lost no time in bringing Mr Plum back to heel. 'You say that you've already heard some details about this incident, sir. May one ask where?'

'Over the bar counter, old son!' said Mr Plum with amiable frankness. 'Soon as we opened at half past ten we had an endless queue of your coppers coming in on the sly for a quick one.'

'And they talked about the murder?' MacGregor pursed his lips disapprovingly.

'Good thing they did!' rejoined Mr Plum. 'Otherwise it might have been days before you lot got around to questioning me. Correct me if I'm wrong, squire, but aren't you up a bit of a gum tree with this one?'

'In what way?' asked MacGregor cautiously.

'Well, like your colleagues calling the girl " Miss X ". I mean, that speaks for itself, doesn't it? You obviously know damn all about her. Right? Not her name or where she comes from or even – if it comes to that – how long she's been lying dead in old Sir Percy's front garden.'

'We're only just beginning our investigations,' protested MacGregor. 'Still, if you can help us in . . .'

'I don't know who she is or where she lives,' said Mr Plum, 'but I do know when she arrived in Frenchy Botham.'

'You do?' In his excitement MacGregor underlined Mr Plum's name twice in his notebook. 'When?'

'Here, hold your horses!' Mr Plum had got his story all worked out and the last thing he wanted was a lot of questions confusing him. 'I'll tell it in my own way, right? Then you can ask me anything I've left out at the end. Now, it was about seven o'clock, as I recall, and I was just having one of my periodic strolls round the bars to check that everything was ship-shape and Bristol fashion before the evening rush got under way. That's how I happened to be in the Public when this girl came in. Real white trash, she was. Blue jeans, a denim jacket, one of those bag things like old sacks slung over her shoulder. Skinny as a rabbit. Long hair all over the place and a good wash wouldn't have come amiss, either.'

'Age?' asked MacGregor, feeling that in spite of Mr Plum's injunction it was time he asserted himself.

Mr Plum paused, more for dramatic effect than because he didn't know the answer. 'Eighteen,' he said. 'Nineteen at the most. And you can take my word for it. My licence depends on me being able to spot how old these dratted teenagers are. Well, normally I wouldn't have bothered with this kid but Toby – he's my barman in the Public – was busy stacking crates of brown so, since I was there, I wished her my usual hospitable good-evening and asked her what she wanted. By the way,' – Mr Plum frowned behind his whiskers. Trying to remember every blessed detail was proving trickier than he'd thought – 'did I mention that she was wet? Not too wet, of course.'

'And what the hell's that supposed to mean?' Not *all* of Dover's attention was being given to squeezing the last cup out of the pot.

Mr Plum was more than delighted to explain. 'Well, since I heard she'd been found murdered, I naturally got to thinking about her,' he said. 'And wondering how she'd got to Frenchy Botham. We don't have any trains, you see, since they closed the line ten years ago, and hardly any buses. None that'd get her here at that time of night, anyhow. On the other hand, if she'd come in her own car, even the police would have found it by now, wouldn't they? A strange car, parked all this time in a small village ... Well, that's when I started thinking about walking.'

'I wish you would!' growled Dover in an aside pitched to be heard.

'And *that's* why I mentioned her being wet, but not too wet.' Mr Plum seemed to be expecting some kind of response and was obviously disappointed when it didn't come. 'It was raining cats and dogs that night, you see,' he continued sullenly. ' If she'd done the three miles from Chapminster, say, on foot, she'd have been soaked to the skin. But, like I said, she was just wet.'

MacGregor didn't like being rude to people. 'And what's your explanation, sir?' he asked out of the kindness of his heart.

'I came to the conclusion that she'd been hitch-hiking. She probably got to Chapminster by train or coach and then got a lift from a passing motorist or lorry driver as far as Frenchy Botham.'

Dover proceeded to wipe the smile of quiet satisfaction right off Plum's face. ''Strewth,' he said disgustedly, 'she could have hitch-hiked from Timbuktu for all you know. Or landed from a bloody flying saucer. Or been driven here by her murderer who knocked her on the head and drove away again. There could be a thousand explanations. Look,' – having eaten and drunk everything in sight, Dover was beginning to get bored – 'speed it up, will you? Stick to the facts and leave the clever stuff to us.'

MacGregor hastened to smooth things over as Mr Plum seemed to be turning a rather appropriate colour. 'You asked the girl what she wanted,' he prompted.

'That's right,' agreed Mr Plum sourly. He was taking a good hard look at Dover, as if seeing for the first time what an ill-natured, scruffy old devil he really was. 'Yes, I asked her what she wanted – meaning to drink, of course – and she says can I tell her where The Grove is. No "please" mind you. Kids, these days! Well, to cut a long story short, I told her. Simple enough. Out of the pub, turn right and The Grove's the second road on the left. Five minutes walk and you can't miss it. She thanked me, turned on her heel and walked out.'

MacGregor studied his notes. 'Did you see her again?'

'No. But it is her, isn't it? I mean, the description fits and everything, doesn't it? I know,' explained Mr Plum a trifle obscurely, 'one of the sergeants who saw the body.'

It is not a detective's job to answer questions, and MacGregor ignored those from Mr Plum. 'And she definitely had a hand-bag?'

'Definitely.'

'And when was it exactly that you saw this girl?'

'Ten days ago,' said Mr Plum without hesitation. 'Wednesday, the twelfth.'

Dover stuck his oar in again. Although he was always complaining about witnesses who could never remember anything, he got highly suspicious about those who did. 'You must get thousands of people in your boozer,' he said accusingly. 'How come you've got this girl so clear in your mind?'

Mr Plum could almost feel the noose being slipped over his head. 'I don't quite know,' he admitted uneasily. 'Of course, we don't see that many unaccompanied young girls of her age coming in. More's the pity, eh?' This feeble attempt at humour fell on four very stony ears. Mr Plum hurried on. 'I think it must have been her asking about The Grove that made me remember her. I mean, The Grove's very posh. All good solid houses standing in their own grounds. Not her style at all. I did keep my ears open for the next couple of days or so, in case there was any gossip going around. But there wasn't. Then I forgot all about her until this body turned up.'

MacGregor looked across at Dover to see if he'd had enough. If the scowl and the protruding bottom lip were anything to go by, he had. 'Well, thank you very much, Mr Plum. You've been a great . . .'

But Mr Plum couldn't afford to be brushed off like that. He'd got his customers to think of. They'd expect him to be hand-in-glove with these Scotland Yard detectives and in a position to retail all the news straight from the horse's mouth. 'You do see what this means, don't you?' he asked anxiously. 'It's not just accidental that her body was found in The Grove. She was visiting somebody there and, if you ask me, whoever that somebody was, they're the ones who killed her. It narrows your investigation down to no more than five houses! You don't have to go looking over the entire country for your murderer. He's right here, in this village. In one *road* in this village! Why, there can't be more than a dozen people who . . .'

'What time's supper in this dump?' If there was one thing

Dover couldn't stand it was amateur detectives trying to muscle in on the act.

It took Mr Plum a second or two to get his bearings again. 'Well, whenever you like, squire. Likewise with all your meals. Inspector Walters warned us when he booked your rooms that food would be a problem, what with you keeping such irregular hours. He said you'd be working so hard that you'd just have to snatch your meals as and when you could.'

Dover's face crumpled in a grimace of shock and horror. 'With my stomach?' he howled indignantly. 'What are you trying to do? Finish me off? Now, listen, mate,' – he addressed Mr Plum with more concern and involvement than he'd shown throughout the entire interview – 'and get this straight! I don't want any messing about with my meals. Savee? I want 'em hot, nourishing, on the dot – and plenty of 'em. 'Strewth, it's the only thing that keeps me going, is food! You wouldn't believe what a sensitive stomach I've got. I've had Harley Street specialists weeping over it – and I'm damned if I'm going to have you buggering it up!'

Mr Plum backed off as far as he could get. 'Dinner's at seven,' he said humbly. 'The wife was going to give you lobster patties followed by Beef Stroganov, with apple fritters and cream for afters. But, if you'd sooner have a milk pudding or ...'

'That'll do fine!' said Dover, brightening up considerably at the prospect. 'And I'll take a pint of your best bitter to swill it down with!'

Mr Plum correctly concluded that the official part of his interview was at an end and he reverted smoothly to his role of genial mine host. 'Talking of beer,' he said, 'I hope you'll be able to find time to partake of a jar or two in the bar this evening? A number of my regulars would, I know, be delighted to make your acquaintance. It's not every day that The Laughing Dog is honoured by the presence of one of Scotland Yard's Murder Squad. One or two of my customers have, actually, already indicated that they would like to commemorate the occasion by really pushing the boat out. If you find you can spare the time, that is,' he added hopefully.

For once, Dover was all smiles. 'Oh, I can spare the time all right!' he said.

On the following morning Dover's face presented a somewhat more sombre picture. The clientele of The Laughing Dog were well known in the district for their open-handed generosity, and Dover was now paying the price. It was a good thing that Pomeroy Chemicals couldn't see him. Grey, shaky, a mouth like the banks of the Thames at low tide on a hot day, and a splitting head, he showed a marked reluctance to move any distance away from the nearest lavatory. It was ten o'clock before MacGregor could coax him out of bed and gone eleven before Scotland Yard's finest could be induced to poke a toe into the great big world outside.

'It's less than two minutes by car, sir,' said MacGregor, holding out Dover's overcoat as enticingly as he could.

'It must have been that stuff they gave us for supper,' whined Dover pathetically as he groped for the armholes. 'All that foreign sauce muck!'

MacGregor nerved himself and removed Dover's bowler hat from the hook behind the door with his bare hands. 'I did think that perhaps the third helping was something of a mistake, sir,' he said. 'Especially with your nervous stomach.'

If there was any hint of sarcasm in these remarks, Dover was too far gone to notice it. 'I just hope I can keep that bacon and egg down,' he grumbled as he allowed MacGregor to shepherd him towards the door. 'Here, steady on! There's no need to rush me!' He rubbed one flaccid hand wearily across his face. 'Where the hell are we going anyhow?'

'To the house where the girl's body was found, sir.'

Dover gulped. 'If I have to look at any more bloody stiffs,' he promised, 'I'll not be answerable for the consequences.'

MacGregor was able to reassure him. 'The body was removed yesterday, sir. We're only going to see the occupant of the house – Miss Henty-Harris.'

Dover nodded, and immediately regretted such rash behaviour. 'And I don't have to walk?'

'Only as far as the car, sir. Inspector Walters is letting us have one, and a driver, for as long as we need.'

Dover was concentrating on getting to the head of the stairs. ''Strewth,' he whimpered as, with MacGregor's assistance, he began the long descent, ' I wish I was bloody dead!'

Funnily enough, although Miss Charlotte Henty-Harris looked and acted like one of the leading ladies from Cranford, she knew a man with a jumbo-sized hangover when she saw one. Clucking compassionately, she helped MacGregor manoeuvre Dover across the threshold of Les Chênes and into a comfortable armchair by the drawing room fire.

'Poor boy!' cooed Miss Henty-Harris as she leaned forward and unscrewed Dover's bowler hat from his head. ' What you need is a nice glass of my rhubarb and parsley cordial.'

'What I need,' retorted Dover in a feeble attempt to regain his old ungraciousness, 'is a bloody week in bed!'

'Of course you do, dear!' agreed Miss Henty-Harris with a sweet smile. 'But you've got work to do, you see. Important work. We can't have you laid up just at this moment, now can we? So, you just sit well back while I go and mix you up a draught of something that will bring the roses back to your cheeks. We'll soon have you your old merry self again!'

'Who the hell is she?' demanded Dover as Miss Henty-Harris bustled off happily to her kitchen. 'Whistler's bleeding grandmother?'

'She's the lady who found the girl's body, sir,' said MacGregor with as much patience as he could muster. Well, you did get a bit cheesed off with saying everything three times and even then the old fool didn't know what you were talking about. 'It was in her shrubbery behind the front gate that ...'

'I do wish you'd belt up for a bit,' moaned Dover, letting his head sink back into the cushions of his chair. 'Why don't you read your notebook or contemplate your navel or something, and let me get a bit of rest, for God's sake?'

But there is, as we know, no rest for the wicked, and Dover's puffy eyelids had barely drooped over his equally puffy eyes when Miss Henty-Harris came trotting in again. All the ingredients for her concoction were ready to hand in her kitchen and this, coupled with a rather lengthy experience of mixing the stuff, accounted for the speed of her return.

'Just drink it right down, dear!' she advised as Dover, understandably, shied away from the evil-smelling brew.

'What the hell is it?'

'Never you mind, dear!' chuckled Miss Henty-Harris. 'You get it swallowed down! Hold your nose if you can't stand the smell.'

Since Dover reckoned he was in extremis anyhow, he did as he was told and, though no instant miracle took place, he did gradually begin over the next half hour or so to feel better. Not better enough, of course, to conduct the examination of Miss Henty-Harris himself, but well enough to listen quite intelligently to MacGregor doing the job for him.

Miss Henty-Harris began by describing how she had come to find the dead body of the unknown girl. 'I was going away for a little holiday,' she explained, almost apologetically. 'Just for a week. To a cousin in North Wales. She'd wanted to take me back with her when she came over to the funeral but, of course, there was far too much clearing up to be done here for me to leave then.'

'That's the funeral of your uncle, Sir Perceval Henty-Harris?' questioned MacGregor who had sat up late the previous night studying the notes provided for him by the local police.

'That's right,' agreed Miss Henty-Harris cheerfully. 'We had the funeral on the Saturday, which was very nice because it meant that a lot more people could come. The village church was absolutely packed. Uncle Percy would have liked that. He liked to be appreciated. Of course, it meant a great deal of work for the rest of us because a simply enormous crowd came back to the house afterwards. I thought at one time we were going to run out of food. Relations, mostly, of course. None of them had been down here for years and years and I think they wanted to see if there'd been any changes. There hadn't, of course. Uncle Percy couldn't bear changes of any sort, especially as he grew older. Do you know, sergeant, I had to take all his sweets out of those nasty plastic bags they sell them in these days and put them in little white paper-bags. Little white paper-bags were what he was used to, you see. And they're getting very hard to find, I don't mind telling you. I managed to collect about half a dozen, but I have to keep ironing them. Had to,' she corrected herself with a happy little smile. 'Lots of the silly, time-wasting things I had to do are finished with now, thank goodness.'

MacGregor tactfully reintroduced the question of the dead body and its discovery.

Miss Henty-Harris blinked her baby-blue eyes. 'Oh, haven't I told you about that yet? Well, I was very busy after the funeral, tidying things up and sorting things out. Uncle Percy was a terrible hoarder, you know, and that didn't make things any easier. Then there were bills to pay and certificates to get and people to notify. So it wasn't until yesterday that I felt I could get away to my cousin in North Wales with a clear conscience. Several other people had asked me to go and stay, you know. So kind after all these years. But my cousin in North Wales was the first, so that's why I was going to go and stay with her.' Miss Henty-Harris caught MacGregor's despairing eye and giggled shame-facedly. 'Oh, dear, am I rambling on again, sergeant? I'm so sorry! It's not having had anybody to talk to all this time. Uncle Percy just wanted a *listener*, you see. And then he got so deaf that it wasn't really worth . . . Oh, well, that's all over and done with now. So – where was I? Oh yes, well, I was a bit worried about leaving the house empty, you know. I mean, it never had been before, not in all the thirty years I've been living here with Uncle. He had this *thing*, you know, about sleeping in his own bed and . . .' She pulled herself up again with a rather touching moue of dismay. 'Well, I took every precaution. I sent the silver to the Bank, put the best china out of sight in the cellar, turned off the gas and the water and the electricity, stopped the newspapers and the milk, told the police and asked the Boneses to keep an eye on things in general. They live opposite, you see, and they're always pottering about what with the children and everything and . . .' Miss Henty-Harris was quite incorrigible, but she did keep trying. She took a deep breath and started again. 'So, yesterday morning I was all set to go. I'd done my packing, booked my train ticket and provided for every eventuality ... I thought! It was only when I was actually in the taxi and he was turning out into the road that I suddenly thought about the gate and how I'd really better close it. It came to me, just like that! I don't know why because I can't remember the last time that gate was shut, if ever. Anyhow, I thought it would make the whole place look more secure so I told the taxi driver to stop and I got out. Well, I found that I couldn't *pull* the gate closed. It was all sort of jammed up, you see, with dead leaves and gravel and goodness knows what. The hinges were rusty, too. So I went round to the other side of the gate, in amongst the bushes in the shubbery, to get behind it and *push* it. I'd allowed ample time to get to the station, you see, so I wasn't really worried about missing my train or anything. And, then, there she was, poor child. Just lying there. All huddled up and sort of crumpled. I knew right away that she was dead. Well, you do, don't you? And do you know, sergeant, what my very first reaction was?' Miss Henty-Harris shook her head reproachfully. 'I'm almost ashamed to tell you, I really am. I thought – thank goodness Uncle Percy isn't here to see this. He'd have gone *mad*! He really would. If there was one thing he simply couldn't stand it was having people take advantage of his good nature.'

3

The silence which descended upon the drawing room when Miss Henty-Harris went off to make some coffee was almost too precious to break, but MacGregor felt that he really had to rouse Dover from a meditation so profound that it was beginning to look suspiciously like outright sleep. 'Er – have you any questions that you'd like to ask, sir?'

In normal circumstances an enquiry like that would have sparked off some glittering repartee but, in spite of Miss Henty-Harris's hair-of-the-dog, on this occasion Dover couldn't summon up anything more memorable than a sickly swivel of his bloodshot eyes and a belch.

'I've just got a couple more myself,' said MacGregor, refusing to notice this latest manifestation of Dover's abdominal problems, 'and then I think we can move on to the next people on our list. I don't really see Miss Henty-Harris as our murderer, do you, sir?'

No, Dover didn't, but it went against all his finer instincts to agree with his sergeant. 'You never can tell with women,' he grunted at his most piggish.

MacGregor looked up in amazement. 'But what possible motive could she have had, sir?'

'That's for you to find out, laddie!' Dover sighed and let his eyelids, plus everything else, sag downwards.

Miss Henty-Harris returned with the coffee. 'Now, don't force yourself, dear!' she advised Dover as she deposited the plate of hot buttered scones right by his elbow. 'If you don't feel like eating anything, don't! I shan't be offended. I only brought a little snack along out of force of habit, really. Uncle Percy always liked to have a little something to chew on with his elevenses. And now, sergeant' – she took up her own coffee and resumed her seat on the sofa – 'is there anything more I can tell you?'

'Did you know the dead girl, Miss Henty-Harris?'

'Oh, good heavens, no!' Miss Henty-Harris's reply was vigorous and unequivocal. 'I'm certain I'd never ever seen her before. Unless' – she hesitated – 'unless she'd been on the television, of course.'

'Have you any reason to think that she was?' asked Mac-Gregor, wondering if some promising avenue of investigation was about to open up before them.

'Oh, no,' said Miss Henty-Harris with her usual smile. 'It's only that Frenchy Botham is such a stuffy, respectable sort of place. We simply don't seem to have teenagers like the dead girl knocking around. Or not more than one or two. That's why I thought, if I ever had seen her, it was more likely to have been on the telly rather than in real life. That's where I've had to go, you see, for all my information about the seamier side of things. Up till now, of course. Now that Uncle's gone, I hope to be able to travel around a bit and see all this degeneracy they keep talking about for myself.'

MacGregor decided to forget about the television line of enquiry. 'I believe you acted as companion to Sir Perceval for a number of years?'

'Getting on for thirty,' agreed Miss Henty-Harris with little sign of nostalgia and even less of enthusiasm. 'And, believe me, dear, it seems a lot longer. Companion's not the word I'd use, either. Secretary, nurse, cook, housemaid, general dogsbody and whipping boy – that's what I was.'

'So you weren't exactly heart-broken when Sir Perceval died?'

'I was not!' said Miss Henty-Harris shortly.

Dover leaned forward to collar the last buttered scone. 'Who gets the money?'

Miss Henty-Harris jumped. 'What money?'

Dover encircled the drawing room with a greasy wave of his hand. 'All this lot!' he explained. 'Whacking big house, posh furniture, choice knick-knacks! Don't try telling me the old josser died a bloody pauper.'

'Of course he didn't,' admitted Miss Henty-Harris. 'Uncle Percy was a very rich man.'

'So, who gets it?' repeated Dover who, although he had every reason to be grateful to Miss Henty-Harris, wasn't.

'Really, you're almost as bad as my relations,' she said rather crossly. 'Uncle Percy left everything to me. And why shouldn't he? Dear heavens, I've earned it! Putting up with him with his meanness and his bad temper and his tantrums and all the rest of it for nearly thirty years. And for a mere pittance. "You'll have it all when I'm gone, Charlotte," he used to say. Well, now he has gone and I have got it and I mean to enjoy myself with it.' Miss Henty-Harris drew herself up, clamped her mouth shut in a hard line and folded her arms defiantly. She looked a little too much like a thwarted hamster to carry total conviction, but there was no mistake but that these questions about the disposal of Sir Perceval's estate had got her on the raw.

Dover, meanwhile, was definitely perking up. Miss Henty-Harris's ministrations had done their work and he began to flex his muscles. After all, as he himself frequently said, why start mixing it with sixteen-stone desperadoes when there are lots of widows and orphans and frail little old ladies just asking to be shoved around. He got down to brass tacks with a crudity that brought the tears to MacGregor's eyes. 'What did this old geezer die of, anyhow?'

'He died of old age,' said Miss Henty-Harris stiffly. She was beginning to regret a number of kindnesses in the recent past. 'He was ninety-one years old and even Knights of the British Empire cannot expect to live for ever.'

'Where did he kick the bucket?' Dover was away now like a house on fire.

'Where? Why, here, of course. In this house. In the dining room if you want the precise location. We had it fitted up as a bedroom for him some fifteen years ago to save all that traipsing up and down the stairs.'

'Anybody with him at the time?'

'I was!' snapped Miss Henty-Harris who had caught the drift of Dover's questions and didn't like it. 'It happens to be quite impossible to engage a night nurse in this area. They won't come for love nor money.'

Dover's boot-button eyes narrowed. He'd still got the remnants of a headache lurking around in his skull, but he was stoutly determined to carry on. If he could actually arrest a killer within less than twenty-four hours of ... 'Strewth, the mind boggled! Pomeroy Chemicals Limited would have to sit up and take notice of that, all right! Dover dragged his mind away from four-figure expense accounts and keys to the Executives' washroom, and put the boot in with practised skill.

Miss Henty-Harris was outraged. 'How dare you?' she spluttered, the carmine mounting in her quivering cheeks. 'I thought you were supposed to be investigating a murder, not making extremely unpleasant allegations about me.'

'Depends on whose murder we're talking about, missus.'

'I beg your pardon?'

'Look at it from my point of view,' invited Dover with every appearance of being reasonable. 'Here's an old geezer who's left you all his money, and there's the two of you, all alone at night in this house. Then – surprise, surprise! – the old fellow goes swinging through the pearly gates. Well, what's anybody in their right mind going to think, eh?'

'Not, I hope,' riposted Miss Henty-Harris tartly, 'that I murdered my uncle after looking after him with unstinting devotion since the end of the Second World War. I've a good mind to sue you for slander!'

'I'm merely putting a hypothetical case,' said Dover, marvelling – and not for the first time – how women would always start taking things personally. 'You've got to remember,' he added, making a little joke of it, 'that I'm paid to be suspicious.'

'You're not paid to be insulting!' snapped Miss Henty-Harris. 'Now, if you have any further questions to ask about the girl I found dead in my front garden, I shall be pleased to answer them. If not ...' She gestured curtly in the direction of the door.

Dover flopped back in a sulk and left it to MacGregor to get the interview back onto a more amicable footing. 'I wonder, Miss Henty-Harris,' MacGregor began, switching on the winsome, little-boy-lost smile that usually went down so well with elderly maiden ladies, 'if you could possibly cast your mind back to a week last Wednesday. That would be the twelfth, actually. Er – were you at home that evening?'

Miss Henty-Harris was patently not succumbing to the Mac-Gregor charm. 'I find your question extremely tasteless, sergeant.'

'Really?' said MacGregor unhappily.

'Wednesday the twelfth was the night my uncle died. Well, actually it was in the small hours of the following morning that he finally slipped away. I spent the whole of Wednesday evening at his bedside. The doctor had called that afternoon and he had warned me that the end could not be far off. Sir Perceval was quite comfortable and peaceful. There was nothing anybody could do for him except be with him and wait.'

'Of course,' murmured MacGregor. 'It's just that we have reason to think that that might have been the night on which the girl was killed. I was wondering if you had heard anything suspicious.'

'Sir Perceval's bedroom, as I told you, was in what used to be the dining room. It's on the ground floor at the back of the house. It was an extremely stormy night with a lot of wind and rain. I neither heard nor saw anything suspicious. Is that all?'

After this Dover and MacGregor returned to the haven of their police car in some disorder. They installed themselves in the back seat and tried to sort out their differences.

'I really do think suggesting that she'd murdered her uncle for his money was going too far, sir,' said MacGregor reproachfully. 'In my opinion she'd every right to be annoyed.'

'Garn!' scoffed Dover, totally unrepentant. 'She'd got opportunity and motive. What more do you want?'

'But it's not our concern, sir,' said MacGregor, unable to understand Dover's predilection for going off in full cry after red herrings. 'We don't happen to be here to investigate the death of Sir Perceval Henty-Harris. Our job is merely to find out who killed this girl. Now' – MacGregor's voice took on a mildly patronizing tone – 'we don't want to waste time meddling in things that are none of our concern, do we, sir?'

Dover thought quickly. He could be surprisingly inventive at times, especially when jumped-up, snotty-nosed little sergeants began trying to teach him how to suck eggs. He leaned back, folded his arms and stuck several chins out obstinately. 'I reckon the two things are connected.'

'Sir?'

'Look, we can place this girl in this road on the night of Wednesday the twelfth, right?'

'Yes,' agreed MacGregor, frantically searching for some clue as to whither Dover's thoughts were winging. 'That would certainly appear to be the situation, as far as we know it. But there's no indication that the girl was looking for the Henty-Harris house. Mr Plum merely said that she asked her way to The Grove in general. You think that she was actually calling on the Henty-Harrises, do you, sir?'

'Not necessarily,' grunted Dover. 'Makes no odds, actually, as far as my theory's concerned. In fact, I reckon a chance encounter is more likely because old Miss Thingummyjig over there wouldn't have dumped the body in her own front garden if there'd been any connection for us to trace.'

MacGregor, quite unable to follow the logic of Dover's thought processes, chucked in the towel. 'I'm afraid I don't see what you're driving at, sir.'

'Now tell me something new!' sniggered Dover who could have majored in cheap sarcasm. 'Look, suppose that girl just happened to call at What's-their-name's house. Maybe to ask where somebody else lived or something. Well, then she sees something.'

'Like what, sir?' asked MacGregor with an apprehension born of long experience.

'Like old Miss Thingummyjig holding a pillow over Uncle Percy's face,' said Dover, shrugging his ample shoulders. 'The old boy was in a downstairs room. Well, it'd only need a chink in the curtain and God knows what that girl might have seen.'

MacGregor, in spite of his better self, began to see the possibilities. 'Miss Henty-Harris said it was a very stormy night,' he said thoughtfully. 'Maybe the girl knocked at the front door and, when she couldn't get an answer, went round to the back. Where Sir Perceval's bedroom was.'

Dover nodded. 'And there's old Miss Thingummyjig, caught in the bloody act! She wouldn't have much choice, would she? Either she'd got to kill the girl or kiss goodbye to living the life of Reilly on uncle's fortune. I know which I'd bleeding well do.' He gave MacGregor a dig in the ribs with his elbow. 'Well, it's an idea, isn't it?'

It was, indeed. And no one knew better than MacGregor how dangerous it was to let such ideas take root in Dover's fertile brain. It took a long time for anything to sink into Dover's thick skull but, once in, wild horses couldn't drag it out again. And ideas which the old fool had thought up for himself were even more tenacious. MacGregor was anxious to lose no time exposing Dover's hypothesis to the harsh light of day. 'Actually, sir,' he said, 'I doubt whether you could see into the downstairs windows of Les Chênes from the outside. I fancy they're too far from the ground but, of course. we can easily check. And then, would Miss Henty-Harris be so careless as to murder her uncle with the curtains open? She's a bit of a funny old girl, I agree, but she didn't strike me as being stupid. We'll have to look into all this, of course, but ...'

He was interrupted by a sharp tapping on the car window. It was Inspector Walters who, having attracted the attention of the Scotland Yard men, proceeded to join them. It proved to be more of a tight squeeze than he had anticipated as Dover was sprawling inelegantly over most of the available space. Inspector Walters had innocently assumed that the Chief Inspector would make room for him as a matter of simple courtesy, and only found out his mistake when he had committed himself too far to draw back.

'I hope you'll both be very happy!' tittered Dover.

Inspector Walters, perched uncomfortably on Sergeant Mac-Gregor's knees, held a blush at bay by sheer will power. 'I've just had some advance information from Professor Soames, the pathologist, sir, about the post mortem,' he said and decided not to make a full-scale production out of his news. 'The girl was three months pregnant.'

'Ho, ho!' said Dover. 'That makes it a very different kettle of fish.'

'Does it, sir?'

'Well, it means we're looking for a bloody man, for starters,' said Dover, always ready to share the fruits of his long years of experience with his inferiors. 'And a man, moreover, who lives right here in this blooming road. Yes, I've got the picture now. Some over-sexed joker from one of these houses gets the girl in the family way and she comes gunning for him. He can't stand the scandal so – biff, bang! – and over the nearest wall with the dead body.'

'It needn't necessarily be a man, sir,' MacGregor pointed out as he saw Dover prepared to go haring off down another false trail.

'It does unless you know any woman capable of fathering a bastard!' retorted Dover crushingly.

'That's not quite what I meant, sir,' said MacGregor, trying to address Dover across the intervening bulk of Inspector Walters. 'All I'm saying is that, assuming the girl had come to Frenchy Botham to confront the putative father of her unborn child, it still needn't have been him who actually killed her. It could just as easily have been the man's wife, or his mother even.'

'What the hell for?' demanded Dover incredulously.

MacGregor shrugged his shoulders as best he could with Inspector Walters still sitting in his lap and wondered why he bothered. He might just as well keep his mouth shut for all the good reasoned arguments did. 'Well, to protect the man, for instance, sir. Or the marriage or something. Or perhaps out of jealousy. Women do sometimes react quite violently to this sort of situation. They put all the blame on the girl, you see, and ...'

'All I see is that you know as much about it as my old boot!' said Dover disparagingly. ''Strewth, where do you get these ideas about marriage from anyhow? The back of cigarette cards?'

'I was just trying to cover all the possibilities, sir,' muttered MacGregor who, being as yet an unplucked rose, was fair game for the sneers of much-married martyrs like Dover.

'That all?'

Inspector Walters, unused to being addressed quite so savagely, gave a little jump. 'I beg your pardon, sir?'

Dover's heavily jowled face settled into its habitual scowl of discontent mixed with dyspepsia. 'I said, is that all you've got to tell us or are you sitting there waiting for a bloody bus?'

Even Inspector Walters could take a hint when it came wrapped round a brick. Before he could make his escape, though, he had another mission to carry out. He took an envelope out of his pocket and endeavoured to hand it to Dover. Dover, who'd been caught like that before, refused to take it and, after some confusion, the inspector was obliged to entrust the envelope to MacGregor. 'It's just some photographs of the dead girl,' he explained lamely. 'I thought they might come in useful. Our chap's made her look as life-like as possible.'

MacGregor examined the photographs. 'Oh, well, better than nothing,' he allowed. 'By the way, you've got your men making enquiries on the railways and buses, have you?'

'Of course!' Inspector Walters was slightly affronted at the question. He mightn't be a member of Scotland Yard, but he did know his job. 'I'll let you know the minute we get any lead. I can't help feeling that somebody somewhere must have seen her. Oh, by the way, sir' – he turned to Dover – 'what do you want me to do about the newspapers and the television?'

For once Dover had the answer worked out. 'I'll hold a press conference,' he said grandly, already seeing his name in headlines and his face on the box. Pomeroy Chemicals Limited would like that! 'Strewth, if he played his cards right, it might mean another couple of thou a year at least.

Inspector Walters squirmed uneasily. 'Well, I don't think we've quite got enough for a conference at the moment, sir,' he said, eyeing Dover much as a nervous matador eyes the bull. 'The boy from the *Chapminster Gazette* is sort of covering it for everybody at the moment. Mind you, as soon as there are any spectacular developments the big bugs from London'll be down quick as a flash, but they're not actually here at the moment.'

Dover turned nasty. 'Then why ask me what to bloody well do about them, you moron?'

'Actually, it was more about the girl's picture, really, sir.' Inspector Walters knew he was grovelling and was furious with himself but, somehow, he couldn't seem to help it. 'I was wondering if we should distribute copies now for publication in the media or wait till later – in case our own enquiries turned up something. I mean, you know what it's like if we publish a picture and ask people if they've seen the person concerned. We get swamped with replies, most of which are a complete and utter waste of time.'

'I think we'll hang on for a bit,' said MacGregor as Dover, apparently bored out of his mind with such trivial details, stared bleakly and silently out of the window. 'It's early days yet and there's no point in making more trouble for ourselves than we need.'

'No,' agreed Inspector Walters, privately thinking that they'd already got more than their fair share of trouble sitting right there in the back seat with them.

4

In happier and more carefree days it was at this point that
Dover, drained and exhausted by the effort of having done half-
a-morning's work, would have knocked off for lunch. But the
prospect of a highly paid sinecure with Pomeroy Chemicals
Limited was proving a hard taskmaster and Dover determined
to press relentlessly on. He would, he announced to a suitably
astounded MacGregor, conduct one more interview before with-
drawing for a well-earned pint, two helpings of Lancashire hot-
pot and a quiet kip.

'In that case, we'd better tackle the Goughs, sir,' said Mac-
Gregor, consulting his list of people who lived in The Grove.
'I understand Mrs Esmond Gough has a preaching engagement
this afternoon.'

'Mrs Esmond Gough?' Dover wasn't good at names but this
one rang a faint bell.

'That's right, sir. She's the woman who wants to be a bishop.'
MacGregor tucked his notebook away and reached for the door
handle. 'I expect you've seen her on the telly. She's always
coming on these chat shows and what-have-you. She's running
this terrific campaign for having women priests and they say she's
dead set on being the first woman bishop in England.'

'Oh, that nutter!' snorted Dover disparagingly. As a card-
carrying male chauvinist pig, his views on the position of women
were crudely predictable and certainly didn't include having 'em

up there in the bloody pulpit spouting morality at him. 'What she wants is a good belt round the ears. And, if she was my wife, she'd get it! Silly cow!'

MacGregor doubted very much if the man had yet been born who was capable of taking on the formidable Mrs Esmond Gough. She was an athletically built woman in her early forties who had a good brain and the single-mindedness of a steam-roller. If it came to a straightforward contest between her and Dover, she'd win hands down every time. On the other hand, it was not Dover's style to get himself involved in straightforward contests and MacGregor felt that old depression creeping over him as he got out of the car. He'd seen Dover pinning murders onto people he didn't like too often not to be worried about it. In view of the old fool's feelings about women who earned more money and got more attention than he did, MacGregor felt that Mrs Esmond Gough would be well advised to watch her step. He turned to help Dover get out and found some consolation in the thought that even so rabid a proponent of sex equality as Mrs Esmond Gough could hardly be the father of the dead girl's child.

Mr Esmond Gough could, though.

MacGregor was rather surprised to find that there was a Mr Esmond Gough although, now he came to think of it, he had heard Mrs Esmond Gough wax lyrical on the joys of married love on several occasions. Actually, Mr Esmond Gough was a retired brigadier-general, and it was he who answered the door and welcomed the two detectives. He conducted them into a large sitting room which was apparently doubling as campaign headquarters. There were pamphlets and posters everywhere, a duplicating machine, a couple of typewriters and several huge piles of envelopes which the Brigadier had been labouring to address.

'Mrs Esmond Gough will join us in a minute, gentlemen,' he said as he cleared a heap of collecting boxes and files off a couple of chairs. 'She's on the phone to Sweden. We get a lot of support, both moral and financial, from Sweden. They're so much more enlightened about things over there.' As a matter of fact the

Brigadier was far from being a fanatic about women's rights in general or female priests in particular, but he loyally gave his wife one hundred per cent support in her endless campaigns. Not only did this make for marital harmony, but the contributions Mrs Esmond Gough received enabled the Brigadier to enjoy a higher standard of living than his own unaided army pension would have permitted. The Brigadier had something of a taste for the good things in life. He also appreciated his wife's frequent absences from the domestic hearth as she carried out her engagements in every quarter of the globe. With a few elementary precautions, an attractive middle-aged man with a reasonably fat wallet could still find life worth living.

This side of the Brigadier's personality had not, as it happens, escaped Dover who, having sat down heavily on the chair which had been cleared for him, had been making his own moody assessment of his host. He was just the type, Dover reckoned, to go lusting after a kid young enough to be his grand-daughter.

'This is a bad business,' said the Brigadier.

Dover scowled. 'What is?'

'Well, this murder,' said the Brigadier, who'd only been making polite conversation and was disconcerted to find himself apparently in the dock.

'You speak for yourself!' growled Dover with an unpleasant sniff. ' Murder may be a bad business to you, but it happens to be my bread and butter.'

'Oh, quite,' said the Brigadier hurriedly. 'Quite. I – er – I hadn't looked at the tragedy in quite that light before.' He turned, as so many did after their initial encounter with Dover, to Sergeant MacGregor for relief and comfort. Apart from anything else, the younger man was, of course, so much pleasanter to look at.

MacGregor obligingly produced a nice, innocuous question. ' Do you and Mrs Gough live here alone?'

'Yes, we do.'

'No servants?'

'None living in. There's a char-lady who comes in a couple of mornings a week.'

'And no children?'

The Brigadier sighed and shook his head sadly. 'I'm afraid not.' He lowered his voice. 'Things might have been different if we had, I suppose. I mean, whatever else you say about children, they do tend to keep a woman *occupied*, don't they? Fill up the day for her. Give her something to think about.'

'I suppose so,' agreed MacGregor, assuming that these somewhat generalised remarks had particular application to Mrs Esmond Gough.

The Brigadier sighed again. 'Ah, well,' he said, 'it was not to be. My fault, too,' he added despondently. 'Some damn-fool bug I got into the old system out in Korea – or so the medics tell me. Rotten thing for a chap to have to admit to, but I don't care to have people going around putting the blame on my lady wife.'

Dover got bored with all this gruff, soldierly talk. 'Where were you when it happened?' he demanded, injecting a real edge of malice into the question.

The Brigadier failed to fall into so obvious a trap. 'I'm afraid I don't know when the murder was committed,' he said with every show of innocence.

Dover's scowl grew blacker. If there was one thing he couldn't stand it was people trying to be clever with him. He was just about to get really nasty when the door opened and Mrs Esmond Gough made her entrance.

She hadn't, as it happens, been on the telephone to Sweden or anywhere else. That was just a pious fiction. What she had been doing in the intervening moments was working away in front of the mirror, achieving her usual expert job on her face. Some of her more besotted followers might attribute that flawless skin, those sparkling eyes and that well-moulded figure to holiness and clean living, but Mrs Esmond Gough knew that it took a good deal more than that.

She swept into the room in a swirl of diaphanous purple – a colour which suited Mrs Esmond Gough's rather regal personality, and the prelatical connotations of which had probably not escaped her notice. In the last few years, when her campaign for women priests had really taken off and she had started making appearances on colour telly almost every week, she had begun to dress almost exclusively in purple. It had become her trade mark.

'Oh, please,' she said in that wonderfully musical voice of hers, 'do please sit down!'

The two gentlemen who had risen to their feet at her entry duly complied with the request, while Detective Chief Inspector Dover remained slumped in his chair like a sack of potatoes. He was busy trying to get his tongue round a piece of Miss Henty-Harris's buttered scone which was lurking somewhere behind his upper set. It was no good, though. In the end he was obliged to take his teeth right out and remove the offending crumb with his finger.

Mrs Esmond Gough didn't bat an eyelid. She was not the woman to be put out by a gratuitous display of male rudeness. After all, she'd been engaged for a number of years in storming one of the last masculine bastions – and clerks in holy orders can play it remarkably rough when they put their minds to it. She seated herself with deliberate grace in a chair which only the really petty-minded would have found at all like a bishop's throne. 'We won't offer you any coffee,' she announced with a winning smile, 'as I'm sure Miss Henty-Harris has already given you some. My husband' – the word was pronounced with a special affection – 'saw you coming out of her drive.'

The Brigadier made the formal introductions. 'They want to know what we were doing at the time of the murder, m'dear.'

'That would probably be about ten days ago,' explained MacGregor in an attempt to save time. 'A week last Wednesday, to be precise.'

Mrs Esmond Gough glanced enquiringly at her husband. 'Good heavens,' she murmured, 'we shall have to think about that. It's not easy to remember off hand. Perhaps if you were to get my engagements book, dear ...'

'It's the night Sir Perceval Henty-Harris died, I believe,' said MacGregor.

Mrs Esmond Gough's face cleared. 'Ah, that helps!'

The Brigadier blinked. 'Does it, m'dear?'

'Is it the evening you are interested in, sergeant, or earlier in the day?'

'We would like to know about the evening,' said MacGregor. 'Say from about six o'clock.'

'Wednesday was the twelfth, wasn't it?' Mrs Gough had got the problem well under control – and it showed. 'Well, I think my husband and I can provide ourselves with a perfectly satisfactory alibi, if that is in effect what you are looking for. Now, are you ready, sergeant?' She waited calmly until MacGregor, pencil and notebook at the ready, indicated that he was all ears. 'Do stop me if I go too fast for you. Now, on Wednesday the twelfth we had our evening meal rather early. Say about six o'clock. It was actually more of a snack as we occasionally find it more convenient to have our main meal in the middle of the day. When we'd finished eating, my husband came in here to watch the television. He does that every evening, unless we are entertaining guests, so that's no problem.'

The Brigadier grinned sheepishly.

Mrs Esmond Gough went confidently on. 'And I remained in the kitchen.'

'Washing up?' MacGregor recalled that Mrs Esmond Gough liked to represent herself as a highly domesticated woman who loved doing her household chores in spite of the numerous commitments which one might have imagined took up the greater part of her time.

If MacGregor's question had been something in the nature of a little joke, Mrs Esmond Gough didn't see it. 'For a few minutes, yes. Then I got down to painting the posters.'

MacGregor's racing pencil faltered. 'Painting the posters?'

Mrs Esmond Gough nodded. 'On Thursday the thirteenth, as you may remember, we had our Monster Rally and Demonstration in Westminster. We picketed the Abbey and Westminster Cathedral for an unbroken stretch of twelve hours. My organization is strictly non-denominational, of course.'

'Your organization?' MacGregor was asking the question more for Dover's benefit than his own.

'The Sorority for Sacerdotal Sex Equality.' Mrs Esmond

43

Gough rattled off the title with every appearance of pride and satisfaction. 'Known as the S.S.S.E. for short, of course. We are having a Bumper Pray-In at St Paul's next week,' she added, anxious not to waste any chance of proselytizing. 'Everyone is welcome. Gender is no bar. And you may be interested to know that I have plans in the near future for tackling the Eastern Orthodox Church. It is not an institution which impinges upon me personally, of course, but I feel I have a duty to attack and expose all forms of religious sexual discrimination wherever I may find it. The Orthodox Church ...'

MacGregor put the brakes on. If Dover, sitting there with his eyes closed and his mouth gaping revoltingly open, were not yet actually asleep, he'd be beginning to find Mrs Esmond Gough very tedious. Besides, MacGregor still hadn't cleared up this question of the posters. 'You, yourself, Mrs Esmond Gough, were painting the posters?'

Mrs Esmond Gough shrugged as handsome a pair of shoulders as MacGregor was likely to see in the course of that particular murder investigation. 'My Action Committee let me down at the eleventh hour – as usual. Some fool of a woman broke her arm, I understand. Really, some people have absolutely no consideration.'

'You don't have your posters done professionally?'

'No, no! Oh, believe me, sergeant, an amateurish-looking job is much more effective. It looks as though it's a cry from the heart, you see, and it gets the media people talking about "ordinary folk" and "grass roots" and all that kind of thing. I haven't used professionally prepared posters for years. I stick the odd spelling mistake in, too.' Mrs Esmond Gough chuckled ruefully. 'That's usually guaranteed to catch the eye of some world-weary cameraman.'

Dover stirred restlessly. It might have been impatience, indigestion or just a bad dream, but MacGregor took the hint and dragged the interview back to the nitty-gritty again. He addressed his question to both the Esmond Goughs. 'Did the murdered girl call here on the night of Wednesday the twelfth?'

Two heads shook as one.

'Did anybody at all call here that night?'

Again the answer was firmly in the negative.

'Have either of you ever seen the girl before?'

The Brigadier and his lady stared at one of the photographs which Inspector Walters had given MacGregor. The heads shook for a third time.

'Poor girl!' murmured Mrs Esmond Gough with rather slick compassion. 'Poor, poor girl!'

The Brigadier, too, felt the pathos of that wan little face. 'Damned shame!' he growled and blew his nose loudly.

The powerful rumble of Dover's stomach successfully ruined the tribute of a moment's respectful silence which the Esmond Goughs were endeavouring to offer to the dear departed. It probably woke Dover up as well because his eyes suddenly opened and he began smacking his lips as though he'd got a very unpleasant taste in his mouth. Looking round for a bit of innocent sport, he naturally picked on the frailer spouse. 'So you were all alone in this room, were you?'

The Brigadier agreed warily that that was so.

'And the missus was shut away at the back of the house in the kitchen?'

'Yes.'

Dover sniffed contemptuously. 'Some bloody alibi!' he commented before turning his attention to Mrs Esmond Gough. 'What time did you clap eyes on him again?'

Mrs Esmond Gough, who had been stoking up for an explosion of righteous indignation, postponed it and concentrated on answering Dover's question. 'It would be ten o'clock,' she said with a glance at her husband for confirmation. 'Yes, I arrived just in time to watch the News.'

'With our Ovaltine,' added the Brigadier helpfully. 'We have a cup every night and I would certainly have remembered if Moo had forgotten to bring it in.'

'I have the evening quite clear in my mind,' said Mrs Esmond Gough, her natural superiority reasserting itself. 'I finished all the posters and cleared everything away in the kitchen while they were drying. Then I got our hot drinks ready.'

'What were you working in the kitchen for?' asked Dover in a half-hearted attempt to catch Mrs Esmond Gough napping.

'In case I spilt any paint, of course!' Mrs Esmond Gough laughed in a rather mocking way as though surprised that even a stupid male slob like Dover should need to be told that. 'The kitchen floor is tiled and all the working surfaces are washable. One would hardly undertake such a potentially messy job on one's best drawing room carpet, would one?'

Dover, harkening at last to the voice of his inner man who had been talking about lunch for some time, hoisted himself to his feet. 'Come on, laddie!' he said.

Mrs Esmond Gough caught onto the situation with unflattering delight and alacrity. 'Oh, are you going? Well, I'll see you out.' The Brigadier made as if to rise but his wife stopped him. 'No, you just stay there, my dear!' she ordered firmly. 'I'd like you to get on with the envelopes, if you don't mind. We really ought to get them in the box tonight so that they'll catch the first post on Monday morning.'

Once through the front door, Dover was all set for a quick dash to the waiting police car and back to The Laughing Dog, but he found himself being momentarily detained by Mrs Esmond Gough. She was a great believer in last impressions and was quite prepared to cast her bread on even the most unpromising looking of waters. She thought that Dover's heart might be reached by a show of warm, feminine sympathy and touched his sleeve shyly. 'That poor girl!' she murmured again, her eyes moist with unshed tears. 'Have you found out yet who she is?'

'Not yet, I'm afraid,' said MacGregor, hoping against hope that Dover wouldn't resort to physical violence in an attempt to make his escape. 'However, I'm sure it's only a matter of time.'

'And her family!' moaned Mrs Esmond Gough. 'Her poor, poor mother! She's the one my heart bleeds for!'

'Yes,' said MacGregor, feeling inadequate.

'How she must be suffering!' Mrs Esmond Gough gave a little shudder and adroitly brought the conversation back to herself. 'I know how she feels, poor woman, although I haven't of course been blessed with children myself. We had such high hopes, the

Brigadier and I, when we married but, alas, they were not to be.' She dabbed pathetically at her eyes with a very pretty lace handkerchief.

MacGregor squirmed and Dover gawped.

'The Brigadier,' continued Mrs Esmond Gough, looking noble, 'has never reproached me, although at times he must have felt that I have let him down badly. A lesser man might have been tempted to set his barren wife aside as, indeed, the law permits him to do but . . . Oh, well' – she pulled herself together bravely and changed the subject – 'I shall pray for your success.'

Dover could only stand so little. To MacGregor's embarrassment, he shouldered Mrs Esmond Gough unceremoniously out of the way and went lumbering off down the front steps and along the drive. MacGregor was left to make what amends he could for this boorishness. He seized Mrs Esmond Gough's hand and squeezed it sympathetically. Then, with a mumbled word of thanks and apology, he too was away.

5

'Look,' said Dover in one of those exasperated voices that showed he was making every effort to be reasonable, 'why mess about? Let's get a warrant and run the bastard in!'

From time to time Dover could be pretty pungent, even in the open air. In the close confines of the police car, MacGregor was finding him well nigh unbearable. Still, he had to stick it out. He simply couldn't let Brigadier Gough be arrested for murder just because Dover happened to have taken a violent and irrational dislike to the poor fellow and because – more important – the Chief Inspector wanted a quick scalp to wave before the astonished eyes of Pomeroy Chemicals. MacGregor got his handkerchief out and took a long time over blowing his nose. 'But, sir,' he said, 'there is absolutely no evidence. We'd never get a warrant for his arrest, and as for securing a conviction in court ...'

'Who cares about convictions in court?' demanded Dover incredulously. ''Strewth, I'll be sitting pretty at Pomeroy Chemicals Limited long before it ever comes to trial. By then it won't matter a damn what the bloody verdict is.'

MacGregor got his cigarettes out. It was the equivalent of diverting the attention of a fractious baby by means of a sweetie. 'How about a smoke, sir, while we talk things over?'

Dover accepted the cigarette, of course, but he was not the

man to be bribed. Well, certainly not by one lousy, filter-tipped, low tar fag. 'I don't know what you mean – no evidence,' he grumbled. 'For a start, he hasn't got an alibi.'

MacGregor gently pointed out that not everybody unable to furnish a cast-iron alibi is necessarily guilty of murder.

Dover wasn't listening. 'I'll tell you precisely what happened, laddie. Brigadier What's-his-name gets this dead girl into trouble, right?'

'There is absolutely no indication that he even knew her, sir!' wailed MacGregor.

Dover looked surprised. 'But he's got "lady-killer" written all over him! He's bound to be up to something on the side with a wife like that. 'Strewth, it can't be much bloody fun being married to a woman who wants to be a bishop. Now, where was I?'

'You'd got the dead girl pregnant by Brigadier Gough, sir,' said MacGregor, chucking in the sponge.

'So she comes charging all the way out here to ask him what he's going to do about it. Maybe she's blackmailing him or threatening to tell his missus or demanding marriage or wants money for an abortion – I don't know. We can fill in the details later – when we've got His Nibs alone in a cell with no witnesses. I know his sort. All wind and water. It'll not take me five minutes to bash a few particulars out of him.' Dover's lower lip trembled at the prospect of such delights and a lump of ash dropped unheeded off his dangling cigarette to disappear without trace into the antique patina of his waistcoat. 'And the rest of the story's as clear as bloody daylight! Our gallant soldier boy's in that front room watching the telly while her ladyship's in the kitchen painting her silly posters. There's a ring at the front door. She doesn't hear it, but he damned well does. He goes and answers the door – and there's his illicit lady love, spelling BIG TROUBLE in capital letters. Being a man of action, he picks up the nearest blunt instrument, clouts her one on the nut with it and tips the body over the garden wall of the house next door. You've got to admit, laddie,' said Dover, seizing hold of the one hard fact in his whole hypothesis, 'that she was found in the garden of the house next door. Convenient, eh?'

'You could make that sort of case out about absolutely any-body, sir,' said MacGregor wearily. Why not just let the old fool go forging ahead and cut his own stupid throat once and for all? Well, one reason was that MacGregor bitterly resented being tarred by the same brush as Scotland Yard's most unwanted detective. And another was that MacGregor had an awful suspicion that, in the event of any fiasco, he would find that he was the one left holding the baby. It had, he reminded himself, happened before.

Meanwhile Dover was proudly producing his clincher. 'But not "absolutely anybody" would give themselves away like the Brigadier did, would they, laddie? Here' – Dover's air of triumph was quite sickening – 'you did notice that, didn't you?'

MacGregor frowned. He hadn't really missed something so obvious that even Dover could spot it, had he?

'It was when they were talking about not having had any blooming kids.'

MacGregor's frown deepened. 'Oh?'

'You bloody don't remember!' Dover's yelp of delight and one-up-manship would have earned a lesser man a punch up the nose. 'He said, before she came in, that they hadn't any children and that it was *his* fault.'

MacGregor nodded cautiously. 'Yes, I remember that, sir. He said it was owing to some bug or other he'd picked up during his overseas service.'

'I thought at the time it was a damned funny topic of conver-sation,' boasted Dover. 'It was only later when Mrs Who's-your-father was seeing us off at the front door that the penny dropped.'

'Mrs Esmond Gough, sir?' MacGregor's frown of puzzlement was replaced by a gasp of annoyance. Of course! 'I remember, sir,' he began eagerly.

But Dover wasn't going to have his thunder stolen. 'She said,' he interrupted loudly, 'that their marriage hadn't been blessed by any brats and that it was *her* fault. Now, that's what I call a bloody discrepancy.'

In his own, much more refined way, MacGregor could be almost as bloody-minded as Dover. He would go to almost any lengths to prove that the Chief Inspector, as usual, had got it wrong. 'Maybe they were both being self-sacrificing, sir,' he suggested quickly, 'and both trying to take the blame so as to spare their partner's feelings.'

Dover's dandruff-flecked moustache twitched in disgust. 'I've told you before, laddie,' he pointed out sarcastically. 'What you know about married life could be written on a silver threepenny bit and still leave room for the Lord's Prayer. Husbands and wives just don't go on like that.'

'All right, sir.' MacGregor wasn't prepared to argue the point. 'Well, perhaps there's something wrong with both of them. That's not impossible, is it?'

'The odds are six million to one against!' retorted Dover, doubling the number he first thought of to be on the safe side. He knew even less about infertility within marriage than his sergeant did, but he wasn't going to let that stop him. 'No, old What's-his-name was trying to give himself the perfect let-out and his fool of a wife, unconsciously and accidentally, blew the gaffe on him.'

MacGregor thoughtfully chewed his lip. 'In other words, sir,' he said slowly, 'Brigadier Esmond Gough was trying to tell us that since he is sterile, he couldn't in any circumstances be the father of the dead girl's unborn child. And, if he wasn't the father, he wasn't presumably the murderer either.'

'That's it in a nutshell,' agreed Dover. 'It may take you a long time, laddie, but you get there in the end. And that's not all, either!'

MacGregor swallowed his annoyance as best he could. 'No, sir?'

'Why bring up the question of babies at all?'

'Sir?'

'Look, we only found out ourselves about half-an-hour ago that the girl was in the Pudding Club. It can't possibly be common knowledge yet, not even in this village. So, how come the Brigadier knows she was pregnant if he's innocent, eh?'

MacGregor was trying to follow the logic of this. 'But are we sure he did know, sir?' he asked hesitantly.

'Of course he bloody well knew!' Dover's heavy jowls wobbled with exasperation. 'He wouldn't have brought up the whole question of his inability to father kids otherwise, would he? You want to pull your flipping socks up, you do!'

There is no doubt that MacGregor would have gone on trying to get Dover to see the flaws in his line of reasoning, but he wasn't given the opportunity. Their tête-à-tête was interrupted once again by the arrival of Inspector Walters. This time he was careful to remain outside the car and stand well back.

'We've just had a bit of a break-through, sir,' he said, addressing Dover through the window which MacGregor had obligingly leaned across and wound down for him.

'Go on!' Dover flicked his cigarette stub out of the window and was so diverted by the sight of Inspector Walters trying to take evasive action that he quite forgot to point out that break-throughs were no longer of significance. The case had been solved without them.

'Yes, sir,' said Inspector Walters when he was quite sure that all the sparks had been extinguished. 'The ticket collector at Chapminster railway station.' Dover's pasty face remained as innocent of comprehension as ever. 'Chapminster is our nearest town, sir. It's about three miles away. Er – I'm stationed at Chapminster, actually, sir.'

'Bully for you!' drawled Dover. 'And it's my lunch-time so get your bloody skates on!'

Inspector Walters went rather red but he managed to deny himself the satisfaction of planting the toe of his boot where it would do the most ... 'My men have been out, showing the dead girl's photograph all round the area, sir, in the most likely localities. This chap at the railway station recognized her. He can't remember the exact day, unfortunately, but she came off the London train late one afternoon a week or so ago. He probably wouldn't have noticed her, except that she was hanging around after all the other passengers had gone, waiting to get into the telephone kiosk. Somebody else was using it at the time, it seems.

Well, she got in eventually and Mr Brewer – he's the ticket collector – thinks he remembers seeing her leafing through the telephone directory.'

MacGregor's eyes narrowed. 'The directory would contain Frenchy Botham numbers, I take it, sir?'

Inspector Walters agreed that it would. It was comforting to know that there was somebody who appreciated the import of what he was saying. 'Mr Brewer can't actually recall whether the girl made a phone call or not, but he thinks not because, a minute or two later, she was back asking him how to get to Frenchy Botham. He suggested her best bet was a taxi, but we're pretty certain she didn't actually take one. We've had a word with most of the local men. My guess is that she hitch-hiked. There's a bit of a snack bar opposite the station and she may have found somebody to give her a lift round there. All this, by the way, more or less fits in with the time Mr Plum saw her at The Laughing Dog.'

MacGregor glanced at Dover to see if the great man felt like taking an intelligent interest in the proceedings. Apparently not. He was still wide awake though, if the malevolent glare he was directing at Inspector Walters was anything to go by. 'The train she arrived on had come from London?'

'That's right, sergeant. Non-stop apart from Bottlebury and that's little more than a commuters' halt, really. In any case, she didn't get on there because we've checked.'

MacGregor sighed. 'London's a big place. Still, we'll have what enquiries we can made there.'

Inspector Walters was even less sanguine. 'It'll take a blooming miracle to pick up her trail, if you ask me,' he said. 'There was nothing special about her. She looked like thousands of other scruffy kids of her age. Her clothes were all cheap and nasty, too. We've got the forensic team giving 'em the once over, but I don't think they're going to come up with any clue as to where she came from. I'd be happier if we could find that sling bag she's supposed to have been carrying. If there is any evidence of identity, I imagine it was in there.'

Dover shivered elaborately and turned up the collar of his

overcoat. 'It's getting bloody cold!' he complained crossly.

It took Inspector Walters a moment or two to work out that he was being held responsible for the temperature. 'Do you want to interview the ticket collector yourself, sir? I can easily . . .'

But the police driver had received a sharp jab in the back of the neck and Dover was gone, leaving Inspector Walters wondering if perhaps there was something wrong with *him*. He stood in the middle of The Grove and watched the police car drive out of sight in a smelly puff of exhaust and reached a conclusion which many had reached before him. Namely, that Dover was a great, fat, ill-natured, thick-as-two-planks slob!

But, thanks to Pomeroy Chemicals Limited, Dover was really trying. By half past three he was back on the trail again, raring to go.

'Where now?' he demanded, breathless from his exertions at a luncheon which had consisted of two helpings of everything.

MacGregor duly consulted his list. 'We've done Les Chênes and Ilfracombe, haven't we, sir? That's the house where the girl's body was found,' he explained for the benefit of those who weren't as quick on the up-take as they might have been and who needed to be told everything at least three times before it stuck, 'and the one next door. Miss Henty-Harris and the Esmond Goughs,' he added, just to make absolutely sure. 'I suggest we go to Otterly House next, sir.'

'No skin off my nose,' grunted Dover with practised graciousness. He didn't bother to ask who lived at Otterly House but MacGregor told him anyhow.

'It's where a man called Peter Bones lives, sir. With his wife. There are several children, too. Peter Bones is listed here as a Sales Manager. I suppose that could involve him in travelling and being away from home a lot. He might have met up with our Miss X somewhere and got involved with her.'

'And pigs might fly,' observed Dover, the strain of digesting all that food making him even more mulish than usual. 'This it?'

The police car had come to a halt in the roadway opposite yet another of The Grove's spacious residences. Dover eyed the driveway and the flight of steps up to the front door moodily. Why the hell couldn't the silly buggers live in ordinary houses like everybody else?

Mr Peter Bone was at home, having been warned like the others by Inspector Walters to keep himself available. He had been taking advantage of the opportunity to catch up with some work, but he broke off amiably enough and ushered Dover and MacGregor into a comfortably untidy sitting room. He immediately got himself enrolled in Dover's good books by offering his visitors afternoon tea.

'Now, then,' he said when he came back after having popped out into the kitchen to give the necessary instructions, 'do you want to see me and my wife separately – or can we be given the third degree together?'

No doubt Mr Bones was feeling a trifle nervous, but potential suspects should never make jokes about the police. The police have remarkably little sense of humour where their own methods and activities are concerned.

Somewhat boot-faced, MacGregor indicated that a joint interview would be in order.

'Oh, jolly good!' At forty Mr Bones still hadn't quite found his style and hovered uncomfortably between being a trendy young man and someone who epitomized all the good, old-fashioned, solider virtues. 'I expect the kids will come piling in as well, but I don't suppose that matters. They're all far too young to realize what's going on but we make a point of involving them in all aspects of family life.'

There were, as it turned out, no less than three little Boneses, all under the age of four. The baby, Amaryllis, was deposited on a rug in front of the fire while the two older children, Ignatia-Jane aged two and Wayland aged three and a half, made a bee-line for Dover. Both they and their parents were happy and secure in the knowledge that all the world loved kiddies.

MacGregor gave all his attention to the conduct of the questioning and resolutely pretended not to notice what was going on on the other side of the room.

'A week last Wednesday?' echoed Peter Bones. 'I'll have to check with my diary. Wayland, old man,' he called as he got a slim, gold-cornered engagement book out from an inside pocket, 'don't keep putting those rusks in the nice gentleman's pockets, especially when you've been sucking them! Ah, yes' – he nodded at MacGregor as he found the appropriate day – 'well, you can cross me off your list, sergeant! That was the evening we entertained my boss and his wife to dinner.' He chuckled and tucked his diary away. 'And that was a social engagement, I can promise you, that left me very little time for going around and committing murder!'

6

Dover was relieved to hear that disposing of the Boneses as murder suspects was going to be a mere formality. Never much in the way of being a child lover, he was finding the two Bones brats something of a trial and would have brought the proceedings to a much earlier conclusion if the ample nursery tea hadn't proved more of a temptation than he could resist.

MacGregor took down the name and address of Peter Bones's boss so that the events of the evening in question could be confirmed if necessary at a later date.

Peter Bones was wonderfully relaxed about the whole thing. 'The Bickertons arrived at about seven o'clock, or maybe a minute or two later. They came by car, of course. Joe drives to their engagements as a rule, and Alice drives them home afterwards. She's not much of a drinker, you see.'

'She's not much,' murmured young Mrs Bones, 'of anything, come to that.'

'Claws in, my darling!' Peter Bones accompanied this advice with a humourless smile. He turned back to MacGregor again. 'My wife and I were busy dressing for at least half an hour before the Bickertons arrived and we'd borrowed Mrs Plum from The Laughing Dog to cook the dinner for us. These do's are no fun for Maddie if she's got to spend the whole evening over a hot stove.'

'These do's are no fun for Maddie, period!' said Mrs Bones in a sour aside. Her voice softened. 'Wayland, darling, I do hope I didn't see you spitting in nice Mr Dover's cup just then!'

The infant tearfully and indignantly protested his innocence and the matter was allowed to drop. The Boneses didn't believe in nagging. Only Dover seemed to be looking for more reassurance than the child's unsupported word.

Peter Bones was anxious to get on with his story. 'Actually we were making a bit more of a fuss than usual,' he admitted ruefully. 'The truth is that I'm in line for a pretty big promotion and old Bickerton will have the final word. He's told me himself that my work's well up to scratch, but I know he's very keen on executives having a good solid home life at the back of them. He doesn't care for people who go racketing around. It may sound rather old fashioned but there's no doubt about it, a wife and family do give a chap something to sort of work for. They make him knuckle down to it and start thinking about the future. Most big firms these days like to have a look at a chap's home environment.'

'Actually, it's called "vetting the wife",' explained Mrs Bones in a bored drawl. For some reason she appeared to be in the grip of a desire to embarrass her husband, and MacGregor began to wonder if the marriage really was as domestically idyllic as had at first appeared.

'Was there anybody else in the house, sir? I've got you and Mrs Bones, the Bickertons, and Mrs Plum in the kitchen. Is that the lot?'

'Well, the children, of course.'

'I was thinking more of grown-ups, sir.'

'There was Blanchette,' said Mrs Bones, elaborately off-hand.

'Blanchette?'

Peter Bones took time off to glare at his wife. 'Blanchette Foucher, sergeant. She's our au pair girl.'

'Amongst other things,' murmured Mrs Bones.

MacGregor wrote the name down. 'And she was in the house the night the Bickertons dined with you? Did she eat with you?'

'No.'

'Where is she at the moment, by the way?'

'She takes a couple of hours off on a Sunday afternoon. Goes for a walk or something. She should be back in half an hour or so if you want to have a word with her.'

MacGregor made another note and then got down to some brass tacks. 'Did anybody else call at the house that night, apart from the Bickertons?'

'No.' The Boneses' reply came in duplicate.

MacGregor produced his photograph of the dead girl. 'Have either of you ever seen her before?'

Neither of them had.

'Suppose,' MacGregor went on thoughtfully, 'somebody called at the house during the evening. Could anybody have answered the door without the rest of you knowing?'

The Boneses exchanged glances.

'I shouldn't have thought so,' said Peter Bones at last. 'Our front door bell's awfully loud. Has to be because of the row the kids make.'

'It was a pretty stormy night, though, wasn't it? And noisy?'

'Yes,' Peter Bones broke off to warn young Wayland of the dangers inherent in chewing the nice uncle's bootlaces. 'You think perhaps that Mrs Plum . . .?'

'Or the au pair girl,' said MacGregor, watching carefully for any reaction to that suggestion. 'You see, we know the dead girl asked her way to The Grove that evening. That rather implies that she knew somebody who lived here. Now, that doesn't really apply to Mrs Plum, does it?'

Peter Bones wiped his hands down the legs of his trousers. 'But it might apply to Blanchette? You aren't seriously thinking that she could possibly have any connection with your murder, are you, sergeant? Good God, she's barely seventeen and she hasn't been in the country for more than a couple of months.'

'We have to explore all possibilities, sir,' said MacGregor with a sigh. 'Were you and the Bickertons together for the whole of the evening?'

'Yes. Well, apart from the odd couple of minutes or so when somebody disappeared to powder their nose or something.'

Mrs Bones had got down on the rug and was playing with the baby. 'What about when you left old Bickerton alone with the port, darling? He said you were gone for at least half an hour. That would have given him plenty of time to bump into this girl, make himself damned objectionable – he's a founder member of the Wandering Hands Club, sergeant – and kill her. After all, she presumably wasn't married to one of old Bickerton's bright young protégés and so she might have objected to being pawed about by the dirty old lecher and threatened to have him up for indecent assault or rape or what-have-you.'

Peter Bones stared at his wife as though he simply couldn't believe the evidence of his ears. 'Well, you bloody stupid bitch!'

'What did you expect, darling?' asked his wife, her eyes sparkling with venom. 'Unquestioning loyalty to the old firm?'

Peter Bones's jaw tightened. 'I ought to break your bloody neck!'

Maddie Bones tossed her head. 'I'm not sure that's the most tactful remark to make in the circumstances, darling. Not with two policemen as witnesses. I imagine they're already looking for somebody with a totally ungovernable temper.'

'I'm sorry, sergeant!' Peter Bones made an effort and calmed down. He even managed a bit of a smile. 'I suppose I'd better explain what all this is about – before you start jumping to any wild conclusions.'

'That might be as well, sir,' agreed MacGregor, very much the stolid policeman. He checked to see that his pencil had a good point on it.

'After dinner,' said Peter Bones, pushing an astonished Ignatia-Jane away quite roughly as she staggered across and tried to climb onto his knee, 'my wife and Alice Bickerton went upstairs to powder their noses and say goodnight to the kids. Alice Bickerton is very fond of children.'

'She is also very fond of having a good snoop round,' said Mrs Bones dryly.

Her husband ignored the interruption. 'When they came downstairs again, they came into this room where Mrs Plum had laid the coffee out. They didn't come back into the dining room where Joe and I were sitting over our brandy and cigars. It wasn't really a case of "shall we join the ladies" ...'

'Although it may look like it!' put in the irrepressible Mrs Bones.

'... Joe and I simply had a couple of points of business we wanted to discuss and we didn't want to bore the wives. Well, we'd just sort of got going when I thought I heard something outside in the garden.'

MacGregor looked up. 'Something or somebody, sir?'

'Something,' said Peter Bones firmly. 'A loud banging. I asked Joe to excuse me and I went outside to see what it was.'

'Which door did you use, sir?'

'The side one. It was the nearest. Well, to cut a long story short, I found that the wind had blown down part of the fencing and that was what was making all the noise. I saw that, if I just left it, not only would it keep the whole house awake all night, but it would probably finish up doing some real damage. So, I got hold of a piece of rope out of the garden shed and tied the thing up as best I could.'

'How long would you estimate it took you, sir?'

'About five minutes. No more. It was pitch dark and raining hard. Naturally, I finished up soaked to the skin and absolutely filthy. I could hardly go back into the dining room like that so I nipped upstairs, had a quick shower and changed into another suit. When I was presentable again, I returned to the dining room, weaned Joe off the brandy bottle and we joined our respective wives here in the sitting room.'

MacGregor, as was his habit, looked across at Dover on the offchance that he might wish to make some contribution to the proceedings, but the Chief Inspector was fully occupied in a life and death struggle with young Wayland over the last peanut butter and Marmite sandwich. Both protagonists had long since abandoned any pretence to civilized standards and feet and teeth were being brought indiscriminatingly into play on either side. 'Did you explain what had happened?'

Maddie Bones stuck her oar in before her husband had got his mouth open. 'Oh, yes, he explained it all, sergeant! He was most plausible. It's not for nothing that he's a professional salesman.'

Peter Bones hunched his shoulders. 'My wife doesn't believe me,' he said with the air of a man stating the obvious.

With all the food now gone, Dover was beginning to show signs of restlessness. MacGregor attempted to stave off the inevitable by shoving a cigarette between the old fool's lips and lighting it for him. The Boneses didn't allow smoking in their home because of the bad example it set their children, but MacGregor reckoned that Dover ranked as a kind of honorary Joe Bickerton – to whom, apparently, almost anything was allowed.

MacGregor tried to pick up the threads of the interview again. 'Couldn't you have produced the broken fencing to prove that your story was true?' he asked.

'The whole damned thing blew down completely during the night,' said Peter Bones sulkily. He watched indifferently as Dover attempted to fend off his only son with the end of a lighted cigarette. 'Just my luck.'

Young Wayland, much disconcerted by this first encounter with sincere adult ill-will, retired under the television set to plot his revenge.

MacGregor was mulling things over, too. It was fairly obvious that Mrs Bones didn't believe her husband because she thought he'd been upstairs that Wednesday evening having it off with the au pair girl. The point MacGregor was called on to decide was whether or not there was some even more sinister explanation for this absence from the dinner party. 'How long do you think you were away altogether, sir?'

Peter Bones wriggled unhappily. 'Twenty minutes?' he suggested as though wondering how much he could get away with.

MacGregor proved he could turn the screws with the best of them. Well, he hadn't served all those long weary years with Dover without picking up a few of the nastier tricks of a policeman's trade. 'Twenty minutes, sir?' he repeated dubiously. 'Oh, well, if that's what you say ...' He made an entry in his notebook with all the solemnity of the Recording Angel writing in the Book of Life. 'We can, of course, always check with Mr Bickerton.'

Peter Bones licked his lips. 'It might have been a bit longer,' he allowed reluctantly. 'It's hard to tell.' He tried to regain his old devil-may-care attitude. 'I did perhaps take my time a bit because I knew old Joe would be perfectly happy as long as he'd got plenty to drink. He's not the world's most sparkling conversationalist.'

'And neither,' said Mrs Bones with considerable emphasis, 'is Alice!'

MacGregor closed his notebook. It seemed a good point at which to break off the interview. It was slightly unexpected and it left the victim to sweat things out on his own for a little. In addition to which, Dover was ready to go. Having eaten and drunk everything in sight, there was nothing to detain him, especially since he had finished smoking his cigarette and was thus completely at the mercy of the Bones children. Ignatia-Jane had taken over as gad-fly in chief and was currently exerting all her infant strength in an attempt to strangle Dover with a craftily thrown skipping rope.

MacGregor and Dover both stood up at the same time, with Ignatia-Jane taking a very painful tumble in the process, but their immediate escape was impeded by the arrival of a singularly unprepossessing girl.

'I am returned,' she announced to the room at large, slightly parting the curtain of mousy hair which covered her face. 'I tek ze children, yes?'

It was Blanchette Foucher, the au pair girl. MacGregor stared incredulously at her. Was this the femme fatale who had lured Peter Bones away from his dinner party for a touch of the old slap and tickle? Thin, round-shouldered and – as far as one could see through all that terrible hair – stupid looking.

Nobody said anything as Blanchette, whose heavy breathing suggested that one could probably add adenoids to her other charms, slouched across to the fireplace and picked up the baby off its rug. She then collared Ignatia-Jane by the simple but effective expedient of hoisting the child bodily off her feet by the straps of her dungarees. '*Où est Vaylant?*' queried Blanchette in a voice that boded no good to the son of the house. She spotted him squatting down behind the settee. 'Come 'ere, Vaylant! Queek!'

Wayland naturally ignored the summons and Blanchette, with an infuriated oath, bore down on him, managing to tuck both the other children under one arm. This left a hand free for Wayland. Blanchette swooped and grabbed.

'*Ugh!*' A very Gallic scream pierced the air. '*Cochon! Petit sale anglais! Ach, mais comme c'est dégoutant!*'

The sound of a heavy French hand making contact with a bare English bottom rang satisfyingly through the room. The two smaller children, who had been tossed carelessly aside into the settee, joined their howls to those of their brother.

Mrs Bones was already speeding to the rescue. 'What on earth's going on?' she demanded.

Wayland raised a tear-stained and scarlet face to his mother. 'I was only having a wee-wee!' he sobbed before Blanchette's hand descended once more.

Naturally they cleaned Dover's bowler hat out as well as they possibly could. They scrubbed it with hot soapy water, they rinsed it in a powerful germ-killing disinfectant, and they sweetened it with copious drops of Mrs Bones's most expensive perfume. It was all in the mind, of course, but somehow Dover still didn't fancy that hat, and when they finally got away from the Bones's house, he carried it somewhat ostentatiously in his hand.

During the half-hour shambles which had followed the discovery of Wayland's appalling revenge, MacGregor had endeavoured to question Mademoiselle Blanchette Foucher about the events of the fatal Wednesday evening, but it was rather like trying to fry a jelly. A very runny jelly, in effect, as the au pair girl was continually oozing away on the pretext of giving a hand in the purification ceremonies connected with Dover's bowler hat. One of nature's skivvies, she was patently unused to the sight of other people doing the work. And then, to cap it all, the stupid vache had not only forgotten all her English in the panic but couldn't understand a word of MacGregor's French either. In the end MacGregor decided to abandon the unequal struggle and return, if necessary, at some future date with an interpreter. If Mademoiselle Blanchette had been an attractive young woman, MacGregor might have persevered longer. But she wasn't, so he didn't.

A light drizzle began to fall as Dover and MacGregor walked down the drive of Otterly House. Actually this was a vast improvement on the foul weather they had been experiencing earlier in the day, but Dover's constitution was a delicate one and it didn't behove him to take risks. He looked up at the drizzle, and then down at the bowler hat in his hand. It was an excruciating choice.

MacGregor noted his superior officer's dilemma and generously offered a more optimistic view of the tragedy. 'Never mind, sir, it might have been worse!'

Dover's scowl was bleak. 'I'd like to know how!'

MacGregor told him.

''Strewth!' Dover's pasty face went even pastier. 'I'd have strangled the mucky little bleeder with my bare hands!' He reached a conclusion about his bowler hat and clapped it back on his head before the rain could make treacle of his dandruff. 'You know, laddie' – he took hold of MacGregor's arm in one of those friendly, affectionate gestures designed to take some of the weight off his own aching feet – 'it's going to be a real pleasure nailing that little bastard's father! I'm not a vindictive man but, on this occasion ...' He sniggered unpleasantly to himself. 'You'll see, laddie! I'll make What's-his-name rue the bloody day he was born, so help me!'

MacGregor suppressed an unworthy sense of déjà vu as he asked the inevitable question and got the inevitable answer.

'Well, of course I bloody fancy him!' snapped Dover. 'What were you doing back in there? Having a ruddy kip?'

'But, even if he isn't telling the truth, sir, murder isn't the only explanation for his absence after dinner. I can think of at least three other reasons why ...'

'Three other fiddlesticks!' snarled Dover. 'Next thing you'll be telling me that you believe that banging fence yarn! As if he'd go standing out in the rain in his best suit in the pitch dark for half a bloody hour. To say nothing of the fact that he'd got important guests to look after. 'Strewth, he admitted himself that he was sucking up to this chap to get a promotion.'

'That's true, sir,' conceded MacGregor who, with his background, probably appreciated the value of social contacts more than Dover did. 'The presence of Mr and Mrs Bickerton would also tend to militate against what, I fancy, Mrs Bones thinks might have happened.'

'And what's that?'

'I imagine Mrs Bones suspects her husband of nipping upstairs and seducing the au pair girl, sir.'

'Seducing the au pair girl?' howled Dover. 'Have you seen her, laddie? No man in his right senses would try and seduce her. I should have thought even a namby-pamby like you'd have realized that.'

MacGregor swallowed the insult. 'What do you think happened, sir?' he asked dutifully.

'I've told you once,' said Dover. 'He's a commercial traveller, isn't he?'

'Well, a sales manager, actually, sir.'

'Same thing!' grunted Dover irritably. 'They're all as randy as buck rabbits. So, What's-his-name . . .'

'Peter Bones, sir,' said MacGregor, with no hope at all that it would stick.

'. . . gets this girl into trouble and she comes gunning for him. It's as simple as falling off a log.'

MacGregor nodded. As theories go, he'd heard worse – and most of them from Dover. 'The timing's not very good, sir. It must have been nine o'clock at least before they'd finished dinner and Bones went out to mend that fence. The dead girl called at The Laughing Dog round about seven. That leaves a couple of hours to account for.'

Dover brushed such pettifogging details aside. 'She was wandering around looking for the house!'

MacGregor tried another tack. 'There were six people in Otterly House that Wednesday evening, sir,' he pointed out, 'not counting the children. How did the dead girl manage to attract Peter Bones's attention without anybody else noticing?'

'Secret signal!' said Dover who was now really firing away on all four cylinders. Pomeroy Chemicals Limited just didn't know what was going to hit them! 'Whistling or singing a song or something.'

'Or tapping,' said MacGregor as he grasped the possibilities.

'Like I said,' agreed Dover. 'She creeps up to the house, peeps in at the dining-room window and sees his lordship sitting there with that other fellow. She taps out their coded signal or whatever and What's-his-name makes some tom-fool excuse to his guest and goes outside. There the girl threatens him with exposure or demands money or something, so he picks up a stone – or a chunk of wood from that famous broken fence of his – and clouts her one. Then all he has to do is get rid of the corpse in his neighbour's shrubbery.'

MacGregor looked at Dover with something bordering on respect. Really, the old fool had produced quite a logical case against Peter Bones. MacGregor didn't believe in it for one moment, but he was quite prepared to award high marks for effort.

Dover was meanwhile rounding off his thesis. 'The whole blooming business needn't have taken more than five minutes. Mind you, he'd have got himself wet and muddy, like he said. He might even have got some of her blood on him. So, all that about going upstairs for a bath and change is likely true. It'd give him time to work out that story about mending the broken fence as well.'

'Hm,' said MacGregor.

'And another thing,' said Dover, really intent on gilding the lily. 'The only person who could say how long he was actually away or why precisely he left the dining room or anything is this other fellow.'

'Mr Joseph Bickerton,' prompted MacGregor.

'Well, did you notice how many times he mentioned his drinking habits? Damn it, he's already branded the only witness against him as a drunk and discounted any evidence he might give at the trial. Here' – Dover's laborious progress ground to a complete halt as he cast a liverish eye at his surroundings – 'where the hell are we? What are we doing here? Where's the bloody car? Look, laddie, I want a bit of a rest and a think before we start on . . .'

MacGregor gently unhooked Dover's arm and, mounting the last of the steps, seized hold of the large brass knocker wrought in the shape of a snarling cat and rapped loudly on the door. 'Mr and Mrs Talbot, sir,' he informed an astounded Dover in a suitably hushed voice. 'He's a bank manager. He sent a message via Inspector Walters saying that it would be convenient for him to see us at half-past four and he kindly invited us to tea at the same time.'

Dover, who had been all set to hobble indignantly away, wavered.

MacGregor smiled, partly in encouragement and partly at his own cleverness. 'We might as well stay now that we're here, mightn't we, sir?'

7

The way to Dover's co-operation lay through his stomach and he tackled this, his second afternoon tea of the day, with every appearance of benevolence and good-will. Mrs Talbot, presiding with matronly grace over the teapot, sensibly kept his plate well piled with goodies.

Raymond Talbot proved to be a pompous man, full of his own importance as the local representative of the Shire & Eastern Bank. He wielded, and everybody knew he wielded, power of life and death over several very substantial overdrafts in the district. Responsibilities like that impart a certain air to a man.

He took immediate charge of the interview. Naturally he would have preferred to deal with the senior of the two Scotland Yard detectives but, if Mr Talbot had one saving grace, it was that he was a realist. He soon appreciated that he wasn't going to get much in the way of sensible answers out of a fellow whose mouth was stuffed successively with sardine sandwiches, ham sandwiches, egg and cress sandwiches, homemade sausage rolls and tipsy cake. And the way he clutched that bowler hat to him, balancing it precariously on what remained of his lap – that didn't inspire much confidence either. Mr Talbot attributed this particular phenomenon to a deep-rooted sense of insecurity. Mr Talbot had not watched all those programmes about The Mind on the telly for nothing.

'Of course, we've already had the local police round,' said Mr Talbot as he passed the photograph of the dead girl across to his wife with a negative shake of his head. A non-customer of the Shire & Eastern Bank if ever he'd seen one. Probably – Mr Talbot didn't feel he was really being unduly harsh in his judgement – a non-customer at every bank in the country. 'We weren't able to give them any assistance, I'm afraid. However, I understand that more positive information has since come in concerning the probable time of her demise, and concerning a possible connection on her part with this particular area of Frenchy Botham. Plum at The Laughing Dog, wasn't it? Well, I wouldn't have classified him as a fanciful man, I must admit, but I can't help feeling he's got hold of the wrong end of the stick on this occasion.'

'Why is that, sir?'

Mr Talbot looked down his nose at MacGregor. If there was one thing that Mr Talbot disliked it was the way the lower orders threw their weight about these days. There was plenty of time for that sort of thing, Mr Talbot always maintained, when a man has reached a position of authority and standing in his chosen field. 'Why is that?' he repeated rather distantly. 'Well, my dear chap, The Grove is hardly *that* sort of place, is it? Anonymous, pregnant, teenage girls' – he corrected himself – 'anonymous, pregnant, *murdered* teenage girls simply don't, quite frankly, fit into an area where every single property would come on the market at not one penny less than forty thousand pounds. I think you gentlemen must take it from me that people who make that kind of investment in a community definitely don't go around involving themselves in affairs of such a sordid and degrading nature. I shudder to think what would happen to the price of houses if they did. No, I suggest you have another word with Plum. He must have misunderstood.'

MacGregor thought it was about time he got Mr Talbot shunted back onto some more profitable line, but before he could do more than open his mouth the bank manager was holding forth yet again.

'Mind you, I fully appreciate that you have to explore whatever avenues open up in front of you, however outlandish and improbable they may appear. That is why I am prepared to co-operate fully. Now then, it's the evening of Wednesday the twelfth you're interested in, I understand? That's when you believe the girl was killed and therefore the period for which we unfortunate residents in The Grove are being asked to furnish an alibi. Right? Well, luckily, Mrs Talbot and I are in the ideal situation for doing precisely that. We were both at home and in each other's company from half-past five onwards, when I returned from the Bank. I was a trifle earlier than usual because we were giving a small bridge party that evening. We had dinner at a slightly earlier hour, too. Our guests arrived between a quarter to seven and seven o'clock. They all came by car. From seven o'clock onwards, then, we were all continually together until about eleven o'clock when the party broke up. No one else called at the house during that time, and no one left it. You may have noticed as you came in that my front door is liberally supplied with locks and bolts. The back door is much the same, and so are all the windows. In addition I have a burglar alarm which is connected directly with Chapminster police station. This is because, as a bank manager, I am in an extremely vulnerable position. A number of my colleagues have, as you will know, been kidnapped and forced to open their own bank vaults to robbers. I have no intention of allowing that to happen to me and I take every precaution. This house has, with the full approval of my Head Office, been turned into what amounts to an impregnable fortress, and next week I am having the latest model of spy-holes installed in the front door. One cannot take too many precautions. I change my route to and from the Bank every day and you will remember that I insisted upon seeing your Warrant Cards before I permitted you to cross my threshold.'

MacGregor did indeed remember, if only because of the acute embarrassment caused when Dover couldn't find his. In fact, if it hadn't been for MacGregor deducing (in the best detective fashion) that Dover's pockets were probably full of holes, they would never have got into the Talbot house at all. Not that that was much compensation for the pure horror MacGregor had experienced as he plunged his hand down into the Stygian depths of the lining of Dover's overcoat. MacGregor fought down another heave of nausea and resolutely turned his thoughts to happier subjects. Like murder.

'Could I have the names and addresses of your guests, sir?'

Mr Talbot was not unprepared for the request. He had the list, already written out and to hand. Such, however, was his love of his own voice that, instead of handing the sheet of paper over to MacGregor, he read its contents out aloud in a clear voice at dictation speed, thoughtfully spelling out any proper names which might give trouble.

MacGregor got them all down. Mr and Mrs Arbuthnot Quail, The Old Brew House, Chapminster. Mr and Mrs Berkley Rawlinson, Corner Cottage, Pebble Lane, Little Alesford. Mrs Natasha Srednaya, 42b Station Road, Swinham, 16.

'Our usual group, in fact,' said Mr Talbot when he saw that MacGregor's pencil had stopped moving. 'We meet here every other Wednesday, except in August. I contacted everybody by telephone this afternoon and they have all expressed their readiness to provide Mrs Talbot and myself with an alibi, in the unlikely event that the need for one should arise.'

And that, as far as Mr Talbot was concerned, was that. It was only because Dover hadn't yet finished feeding his fat face that MacGregor felt obliged to prolong the proceedings. He asked Mr Talbot for the telephone numbers of the bridge players, much to that gentleman's ill-concealed astonishment.

'You're not seriously intending to contact these people, are you, sergeant? I am a Bank Manager, after all. My word is my bond. I can assure you there is absolutely no need to go pestering my guests on the telephone – or in any other way, if it comes to that.'

'Oh, we most likely won't, sir,' said MacGregor soothingly. 'It's just that, if we do have to, at least we shan't have to come bothering you again.'

Mr Talbot sniffed, raised his eyebrows at his wife and read out the phone numbers in an ill-natured gabble. 'Anything else, sergeant?'

'Er – you played in this room, did you, sir?'

'We did.'

'And you would have heard if anybody had come knocking at your front door?'

'Naturally.'

Dover, having gone through the tea tray like a plague of locusts, leaned back, belched loudly and, bestowing his rosette for a blow-out first-class, unfastened the top button of his trousers.

MacGregor realized that it was time to go.

At least, he pondered, as he supported a now limping Dover down the drive, this was one occasion when the Chief Inspector wouldn't try to pin the murder on his late host. Throughout the whole interview he hadn't opened his mouth except to shovel food into it, and MacGregor doubted whether he had taken in anything at all of the proceedings. But, MacGregor was wrong. Dover had been listening.

'A bloody likely yarn!'

'Sir?'

'Overweight stuffed shirt!'

'You mean Mr Talbot, sir?'

'Who else, for God's sake?' Dover paused to admire the Spring flowers. He also contrived to get his breath back and give his poor old feet a rest at the same time. 'You didn't swallow all that load of old codswallop he was dishing out, did you?'

MacGregor tried not to sound too patronizing. 'Mr Talbot has a pretty solid looking alibi, sir. Apart from his wife, there are no less than five other people who can vouch for him. I'm sure they'll all confirm his story when we get round to seeing them, and there's absolutely no question here of anybody nipping out in the middle of a storm to mend a garden fence.'

Dover grunted and resumed his funereal progress down the drive. 'You play bridge, laddie? Or whist, which comes to the same thing?'

'Er – no, sir. We used to play a lot of canasta at school, of course.'

'My old woman's become a bloody whist fiend recently,' said

c*

73

Dover gloomily. 'Says it makes a nice change from bingo.'

Privately, MacGregor reckoned that Mrs Dover had probably earned all the extra-marital amusements she could get, but naturally he wasn't tactless enough to say so. 'That's very interesting, sir,' he commented brightly, carefully interposing his body between Dover and the sight of the police car waiting out in the roadway.

'Once a bloody month,' Dover went grumbling on, obviously unburdening himself of a long-standing grievance, 'they meet at our house. Coffee and bits of sandwiches with all the crusts cut off, and a cold supper left out on a bloody plate for me. And I have to feed the bloody cat! No wonder my stomach's in the state it's in. Cold food rots the lining like nobody's business.'

MacGregor didn't wish to know that. 'You were talking about bridge, sir,' he reminded Dover hopefully.

Dover was growing bored with the conversation and in his impatience failed to notice that MacGregor was leading him towards yet another garden path. 'You play bridge in fours, laddie,' he said irritably. 'Same as bloody whist. Five's just possible because you can have each person sitting out in turn and it's not too bad. Seven, on the other hand, is a bloody silly number. That gives you four people actually playing and three more sitting about twiddling their bloody thumbs. You can't play any sort of cards with only three people, not properly. And certainly not bridge or bloody whist. I know because my missus bitches like hell when the numbers aren't right.'

MacGregor blinked. Was it possible that even the thought of landing a highly-paid job with Pomeroy Chemicals had sharpened up Dover's thought processes? Could the old fool, armed with his vicarious experience of four-handed card games, have stumbled on something that his highly intelligent, highly present-able sergeant had missed. MacGregor started on the mental arith-metic. Two Talbots, two Quails, two Rawlinsons and a Mrs Natasha Somebody-or-other. That made seven all right.

'Perhaps Mrs Talbot doesn't play, sir.'

'Nobody said she didn't,' objected Dover. 'And it's the same difference. Six is a bloody awkward number, too. And so,' he added, just in case MacGregor was going to pursue the point to its limit, 'is five. Here' – Dover ground to a halt outside the wide-open gates of yet another house – 'where the hell are we supposed to be going now?'

'It's the very last house in The Grove, sir,' said MacGregor as beguilingly as he could. 'When we've done this one, we've done the lot.'

Dover puffed his cheeks out and, almost regretfully, shook his head. ''Strewth, laddie,' he confessed, 'I couldn't eat another mouthful. Not right away. Not without ruining my supper. Mrs Plum's doing cod fried in batter and chips, and I just fancy a bit of fish.'

But MacGregor, who'd learnt something during his long years of association with Dover, had foreseen this bolt-hole and blocked it. He indicated his wristwatch. 'It's nearly six o'clock, sir. Mr de la Poche won't be offering us afternoon tea. It's far too late.'

As usual, MacGregor was right about the social niceties. Clifford de la Poche, owner-occupier of Lilac View, the fifth and final house in The Grove, never so much as mentioned tea.

'Oh, I'm so pleased!' he trilled, the diamond rings on his fingers vying in sparkle with the cut glass of his whisky decanter. 'Naturally one always suspected that this "no drinking on duty" rule was a complete myth, but one couldn't be sure. Now, would you care to add your own water, Chief Inspector dear, if any?' Mr de la Poche set down a triple whisky on the little table next to Dover and then turned, in the most touching and appealing way imaginable, to MacGregor. 'Are you *sure* I can't tempt you, sergeant dear?' he queried, dimpling away like mad. 'Not even with a teeny-weeny drop of the dryest of dry sherry?'

MacGregor silently indicated that he was above and beyond temptation of any sort whatsoever.

Clifford de la Poche accepted the rebuff with a charming pout. 'Oh, well,' he begged, 'do at least sit down, dear! You make one feel so *nervous*, towering there. You're such a *big* lad, aren't you?'

MacGregor sat down, advisedly choosing a chair as far away as possible. 'You probably know, sir, that we're here making enquiries in connection with the death of the young woman whose body was found yesterday morning.'

'*What* a tragedy, dear!' Clifford de la Poche raised two pale, limp hands in lamentation. 'Still,' he added more briskly, 'it could have been worse.'

'Could it, sir?'

Clifford de la Poche twinkled at MacGregor. 'It could have been a young *boy*, dear!' He picked up a massive cigarette box in exquisitely tooled leather and offered it to Dover. 'Do you smoke, Chief Inspector dear? The scented ones are on the left.'

'I take it that you don't know the young woman, sir,' said MacGregor, holding out his copy of the dead girl's picture.

Clifford de la Poche shook his head. 'They all look alike to me, I'm afraid, dear,' he apologized. 'Has she got a name yet?'

'We haven't been able to identify her so far, sir.'

'It's just that, where females are concerned, I'm better at names than faces.'

'I wonder if you could tell me what you were doing in the evening of Wednesday the twelfth, sir? That's a week last Wednesday.'

'The day the girl was killed?' Clifford de la Poche caught MacGregor's sharp glance. 'That's from my charlady, dear. She garners every scrap of gossip and retails it to me at great length over our mid-morning cup of coffee. She's been issuing extra bulletins since we had this murder, of course.' Clifford de la Poche pursed his lips to bring out his dimples. 'Well, I've been thinking a lot about it since I heard that we residents of The Grove are the prime suspects. I was at home all day that Wednesday and, after my Mrs Mop had left at mid-day – her name's Mrs Yarrow, incidentally – after she'd gone I was all on my own-some. I didn't see or speak to a living soul all day. So, there are no witnesses at all, I fear, to my complete innocence.'

'You're sure about the date, sir?'

'Quite sure, dear. It was my day for rest and relaxation because I'd had to go up to London the day before. One does need to recharge one's batteries after a day in Town, doesn't one? That was Tuesday the eleventh. I belong to the Pedlar's Club in Capon Lane. I expect you know it – an awful lot of policemen do. I'm on the Steering Committee, you see, and we have our meeting on the second Tuesday of the month. That's why I'm quite sure about the dates.'

'And nobody called on you here that Wednesday evening?'

'Nary a one, dear.'

MacGregor nodded and closed his notebook.

'Oh, goodie, goodie!' Clifford de la Poche clapped his hands delightedly. 'Thank goodness that's over! Now we can all sit back and have a nice little chat!' He filled Dover's glass again, practically to the brim, and crinkled his eyes at MacGregor. 'Surely you can let your hair down now, sergeant dear, and partake of a wee drop? No? Oh, well, I'll just indulge in a teeny-weeny cherry brandy, since we're having a party.' He draped himself elegantly on the chaise longue. 'And what do you think of The Grove, dears? I hope you've been impressed. We're popularly supposed to be a rather distinguished crew, though I'm afraid Sir Perceval Henty-Harris's death has torn a simply enormous hole in our ranks. How was dear Charlotte bearing up? Mind you' – Clifford de la Poche dropped one eyelid in a roguish wink – 'I always say if there's one thing banknotes are really *good* for, it's mopping up tears. And what about Peter and Maddie Bones, eh? I'm sure you didn't find any *skeletons* in their cupboard! Such a butch boy, Peter. All that muscle and masculine drive. No wonder that dear Maddie has her little suspicions from time to time, though I'm absolutely sure she didn't really interview twenty-seven au pair girls before engaging the oh-so-unengaging Blanchette. It couldn't have been more than twenty.

'And I hope you're not just looking at us boys in connection with your nasty old murder. I don't want to be bitchy, but you know what they say – hell hath no fury and the female of the species is more deadly. If Maddie Bones thought for one moment that it was her darling Peter who had *impregnated* that dead girl of yours, *murder* wouldn't have been the word! She'd have *massacred* her! I do hope that, when you get around to checking dear Peter's alibi with the Bickertons, you'll have a good look at dear Maddie's movements that evening. You might just find that there's the odd ten minutes or so that she can't quite account for.'

Dover seemed to be having some slight difficulty in focusing his eyes, but his co-ordination was still good enough for him to hold out his glass for a refill of the stuff that both cheers and inebriates. 'You seem to know a hell of a lot about what's going on,' he said thickly.

'That's my Mrs Yarrow, dear!' explained Clifford de la Poche with a shriek of girlish glee. 'I told you. And she's even *worse* of a rattle than I am when she gets going. Besides, the whole of The Grove has been running up and down like a flock of headless chickens ever since we heard that one of us was the murderer. Everybody's naturally been very keen to clear themselves by putting the blame on somebody else. There is, by the way, quite a strong party in favour of *lynching* Mr Plum, our unfriendly neighbourhood publican, on the grounds that he's the one who put the black on us.'

'Do you know the Goughs, sir?' asked MacGregor, thinking that he might as well take advantage of Mr de la Poche's propensity to gossip.

Clifford de la Poche rose to the question like a trout tempted by a very exotic fly. 'Who doesn't, dear? Well, not the Brigadier, of course. He only exists to make Madame more credible as a womanly woman. His being around means that she can prattle on about how simply *divine* it is being married and *slaving* away for the wonderful hubbie and all that rot.' Clifford de la Poche rolled his eyes in mock horror. 'That spikes her opponent's guns, you see. They can't accuse her of only wanting to be a clergy person because she's unfulfilled in other directions. That's why the silly cow always uses her married name. Not that the dear Brigadier's complaining all that much.' Clifford de la Poche broke off to select a chocolate from the bon-bon dish before offering them to Dover who, absent-mindedly, scoffed the lot. 'Dear Moo earns quite a lot of money from all her television appearances and lecture tours and what-have-you. I hear she's even thinking of writing her biography now, God help us. Mind you' – Clifford de la Poche's eyes glinted maliciously – 'it's not roses, roses all the way. There are some people who'd sooner see Mrs Esmond Gough *dead* than have her as a fully fledged parson. Did you know that Charlotte Henty-Harris *flatly* refused to let her conduct Sir Perceval's funeral service? She claimed that the old boy would have spun round in his coffin at the mere idea. Mrs Esmond Gough was *livid*!'

MacGregor looked at Dover and wondered if he was going to be capable of walking when the time came, while Clifford de la Poche risked a glance at his charming little Fabergé clock. The minutes were ticking away and Clifford had better things (he *hoped*!) to do with his Sunday evening than spend it pouring gallons of expensive booze down the throat of this great *bull* of a copper. Good heavens, church would be out in twenty minutes and he hadn't even done his nails yet!

Since nobody else looked like making the first move, Clifford de la Poche felt obliged to risk it. 'Well, I mustn't monopolize you!' he said brightly. 'I expect you've got lots to do.'

'Have you any thoughts on the Talbots?' asked MacGregor.

'Oh, over at Castle Perilous?'

'Castle Perilous?'

'Well, that's what *I* call it, dear. For want of a better description. Didn't you notice that dear Raymond is barricaded in there like the Crown Jewels? Not that I know much about it from personal experience, you understand. I've only ever been invited there once. However, dear Mrs Yarrow obliges there on occasion and I'm indebted to her for the description of the defences.'

'Mr Talbot said it was to prevent him being kidnapped and forced to open the bank vaults,' said MacGregor carefully.

'Oh, how sweet!' Clifford de la Poche cooed with delight. 'And how convenient that dear Raymond is a bank manager and thus able to explain all! I suppose that's why they always meet at his house where they're safe from intruders.'

MacGregor was well aware that Clifford de la Poche was watching him intently from under those long, curling eye-lashes. 'You mean the bridge players, sir?'

'*Bridge players?*' Clifford de la Poche's joy was quite uncon-fined. 'Is that what he told you?'

'We did,' said MacGregor, fairly certain that Dover was tem-porarily incapable of claiming the credit that was his due, 'think that seven was a funny sort of number to assemble for an evening's bridge.'

Clifford de la Poche stole another look at his clock. No, really, this was beginning to cut things a bit too fine! 'Would you believe a witches' coven, dear?' he asked before scrambling to his feet and attempting to rouse Dover. 'Because that's what it is. Worshipping Satan and sacrificing black cockerels and dancing naked round one of those *rude* altars.' He managed to gain Dover's attention by smacking him, a mite over-playfully, on the cheek. 'Or holding seances and going in for a touch of table-rapping,' he said somewhat more prosaically. He turned back to Dover. 'Time to go, Chief Inspector dear!' he screamed.

MacGregor had stood up, too. 'Are you sure about this?' he asked. 'I thought a witches' coven had to have thirteen in it.'

'Seven's nearly as good, dear,' said Clifford de la Poche firmly. 'And if your poor girl managed to break in and witness one of their *disgusting* orgies, they'd have to kill her, wouldn't they? A sort of sacrifice to whatever dark, mysterious gods they worship. Have you thought of that? Now, do you think you could take his other arm, dear?'

Between the pair of them, Dover was propelled successfully towards the front door.

Clifford de la Poche, though *bending* under Dover's weight, could always find the breath for talking. 'You ought to consider whether this really is a ritual killing, dear. I know they're sup-posed to cut their victim's throat and let the blood run all over the altar, but maybe that's only black cocks or something. Any-how' – Clifford de la Poche had got his front door open and had manoeuvred Dover and MacGregor onto the right side of it – 'do let me know if I can be of any more help, but phone first, will you? Lovely to have met you both! Nighty-night!'

MacGregor was thus left supporting an intolerable burden of sagging flesh and staring at a front door which seemed as solidly shut against the intrusions of the outside world as that sported by Mr Talbot himself. MacGregor was just debating whether it wouldn't be better to prop Dover up against the wall while he fetched the police driver to give a helping hand when a tiny, but wiry, middle-aged lady appeared apparently from nowhere. In fact she had been waiting round the corner of the house for the last ten minutes, but MacGregor was not to know this.

She took in the situation at a glance and, draping Dover's limp arm round her shoulders, took Mr de la Poche's place as supporter on the sinister side.

'I suppose he's been telling you the old, old story in there, has he?' she panted, jerking her head back in the direction of the house. 'Disgusting pig! Told you he was all alone the night that girl was done in, I'll be bound. Well, you can take it from me, my love, that slimy bastard's a black liar on top of all the other things.'

8

MacGregor, who hadn't been trained as a detective at great expense for nothing, deduced that he had encountered Mrs Yarrow, Clifford de la Poche's charwoman and oracle. The fact that she had a large bottle of washing-up liquid and two tins of Vim wrapped up in an apron may, of course, have given him a clue. Actually, Mrs Yarrow described herself as the housekeeper. The non-residential housekeeper.

'Not,' she explained with a haughty toss of her head, 'that I wouldn't be as safe as houses living-in, but there'd be talk. There always is. Folk just don't believe in these here platonic relations, and I can't say as I blame 'em. What,' she asked as Dover emitted a sleepy hiccup, 'is supposed to be up with him?'

MacGregor was not a liar by nature but there are occasions when the unvarnished truth is inappropriate. 'The Chief Inspector has been over-working recently,' he said, working on the principle that, if you're going to tell a fib, make it a whopper. 'And it was oppressively warm in Mr de la Poche's house.'

'Bloody hell!' said Dover quite loudly, missing his footing as he progressed along the dead straight drive.

MacGregor felt obliged to keep on talking. 'Have you worked for Mr de la Poche long?'

'Long enough,' said Mrs Yarrow, sniffing darkly. 'Not that I'd set one foot over his threshold, of course, if he didn't pay double the going rate.'

'Oh?'

'Dirty animal!' snorted Mrs Yarrow. With approximately half of Dover's not inconsiderable weight pressing on her shoulders she seemed disinclined to say more.

Dover attempted to flourish one arm. 'Up the City!' he bawled.

Mrs Yarrow replaced her hat. 'He pongs of booze,' she observed suspiciously.

'Mr de la Poche slipped and spilt some on his coat,' said MacGregor smoothly, wondering why in God's name he imperilled his immortal soul for so unworthy a cause. 'Er – were you implying by your earlier remarks that Mr de la Poche was not alone on the night of the murder?'

'I might have been,' admitted Mrs Yarrow with some lack of frankness. 'And then again, I might not.'

They had reached the police car. With the driver's boot-faced help, they got the Shame of Scotland Yard bundled into the back. It wasn't a pretty sight, but at least they'd got Dover off the street where his appearance and behaviour would not only have frightened the horses but done irreparable damage to police/public relations as well.

Mrs Yarrow straightened her hat again and got her breath back. 'My lips are sealed,' she announced improbably. 'But, I will say this . . .'

'Yes?' MacGregor was always the optimist.

'You might not be wasting your time if you was to go round to St Columbia's church and cross-question some of those horrid little choirboys.'

MacGregor pursed his lips as he tried to indicate that a wink was as good as a nod. 'You mean that a week ago last Wednesday, Mr de la Poche was not alone in his house in the evening, but had some choirboys with him.'

'Not some,' Mrs Yarrow corrected him as she re-wrapped her bundle. 'One.'

'Do you know – er – which one?'

'You'll have no trouble finding out,' said Mrs Yarrow. 'You just charge Mr de la Poche with the murder and he'll produce the name of his little friend all right. You see if he doesn't. I mean, better go to prison for a few months for *that* sort of thing than get yourself a life sentence, eh? By the way' – her tone became quite sugary as she coyly indicated the bundle under her arm – 'this is *my* apron. I left it by mistake when I was here on Friday.' Since MacGregor offered no comment she was forced to continue. 'I could have left it till I come in tomorrow, of course, but I like to have it clean for a Monday.' MacGregor just smiled. Mrs Yarrow swallowed hard and struggled on. 'And the washing-up stuff I've just borrowed, like. Same with the Vim. We've run right out at home. I shall put it all back, of course. Soon as the shops are open. I just thought I'd explain in case you were wondering.'

Chief Inspector Dover sobered up in time for supper. He usually did. MacGregor had suggested that a cold shower might work wonders, but Dover knew that forty winks on top of the bed would bring him up as fresh as a daisy. He was somewhat overstating the case, of course, but he emerged from the Land of Nod quite fit enough to crawl downstairs and do full justice to Mrs Plum's fish and chip supper.

Over their meal the two detectives naturally talked shop. MacGregor might have preferred a rest from the subject of sudden and violent death when he was eating, but at least the discussion took his mind off Dover's table manners. He briefed Dover about what had happened at Mr de la Poche's house and afterwards.

'I was thinking we might leave this business of the choirboys to the local police, sir,' he concluded. 'We don't want to get ourselves involved in any minor breaches of the law which may have been going on. Our interest should, in my opinion, be limited to seeing if Clifford de la Poche can, in fact, produce an alibi for that evening.'

But Dover wasn't prepared to let Mr de la Poche slip through his greasy fingers as easily as that. Pausing only to help himself to those chips which the fastidious MacGregor had left unconsumed on his plate, the Master Mind succinctly outlined his theory that de la Poche did it. 'Look,' he said through a mouthful of disintegrating potato, 'we can still get him, even allowing for the fact that he's not likely to have fathered that girl's kid.'

MacGregor, following the direction of Dover's bulging eyes, passed over his bread roll. 'How do you make that out, sir?' he asked out of pure politeness. The day he couldn't keep three jumps ahead of an old bungler like Dover, he told himself, he'd pack it in.

Dover replied in a spray of bread-crumbs. 'The girl arrives in The Grove looking for this particular house where her boy-friend lives. Right? So, it's dark. All the houses have got their gates left wide open so you can't read the blooming names without going into the driveway, if then.'

'There are only five houses in The Grove, sir. She couldn't possibly not be able to find the one she wanted. It may be slightly inconvenient to read the house names, but it's not impossible. They're all there.'

Dover scowled and pushed his plate petulantly away. 'All right, she didn't know the name of the house. That's bloody possible, isn't it?'

'It's possible, sir,' admitted MacGregor, 'but rather improbable, really. The point is that, in my opinion, she was looking up the address of her gentleman friend when she was at the station in Chapminster. You may recall, sir, that she only asked the ticket collector how to get to Frenchy Botham *after* she'd emerged from the phone box. In other words, before that she'd only known that lover boy lived somewhere in the Chapminster area, but not his precise address.'

'It's all supposing,' grumbled Dover, never slow at picking holes in other people's theories. 'You don't know that she didn't actually make a phone call and tell him she was coming.'

'No, sir,' agreed MacGregor equably. 'But I do know that, if she did look up the name of any resident in The Grove, she would have found the name of his house in the phone book. They're all there, you see: Les Chênes, Ilfracombe, Otterly House, Fairacre and Lilac View. I've checked.'

'You would!' snarled Dover. 'All right, so she knew the name of the bloody house when she was in Chapminster, but by the time she got out here she'd forgotten it. People do, you know. Not everybody's got a memory like a bloody ostrich.'

'No, sir,' agreed MacGregor meekly.

'When she gets to The Grove, she naturally has to go and ask where Mr So-and-So lives. Anything wrong with that?'

MacGregor shook his head. 'No, sir.' He supposed they owed all this intense mental activity on Dover's part to Pomeroy Chemicals.

'All unbeknowing,' Dover went on, 'she picks on that blooming pansy's house. She rings the bell. "Where can I find Mr What's his-name?"'

There was a pause.

'And then, sir?'

'And then,' said Dover, groping around for the knock-out punch, 'she sees something.'

MacGregor, rather than sit there all night, was prepared to help out. 'Like some improper behaviour between Mr de la Poche and this unknown choirboy, for example, sir?'

'Precisely!' said Dover, relieved to find he hadn't forgotten what he was talking about after all. 'Well, Mr de la What's-his-name knows it's disgrace and prison if he gets caught, even in these enlightened days, so he kills her to shut her mouth and then disposes of the body as per usual in amongst the rhododendrons. I haven't,' said Dover hurriedly as he sensed that MacGregor was about to start nit-picking again, 'worked out all the details yet, but that's the general idea.'

MacGregor straightened his pudding spoon and fork and brushed the odd crumb off the table-cloth. 'What about the missing handbag, sir?'

'What about it?' Dover pretended to be more interested in his afters. 'Here,' he ordered, 'go and give that woman a shout. I don't want to be sitting here all bloody night.'

'I think she's just coming, actually, sir. And the missing handbag is of some importance, you know. You see, we've been assuming all along that the handbag was deliberately removed to conceal the identity of the dead girl.'

'Well?'

'Well, if the girl was murdered by Mr de la Poche just because she'd accidentally seen something compromising, why should he go to any trouble to hide who she was. There was no point, as far as I can see. On the contrary, since he had absolutely no connection with her, it might have been marginally to his advantage if her identity were known.'

Luckily Dover could destroy that kind of logic with one hand tied behind him. 'He got rid of the handbag just to confuse us, laddie! To make it look as though she'd been bumped off by the chap who'd got her into trouble—see?'

MacGregor hated doing it of course but he steeled himself. 'Clifford de la Poche couldn't possibly have known she was pregnant, sir,' he pointed out gently. 'Much less that one of his neighbours was responsible or that ...'

Mrs Plum came banging in from the kitchen with a pleasingly loaded tray and Dover's interest in talk about work dropped sharply to zero.

'Well, it's just a coincidence that the bloody handbag's missing,' he snapped. 'An accident.' He watched carefully to see that he got the larger of the two plates of pudding. 'In any case I've been thinking it over. I can't see that it matters a damn which one of 'em we pin it on, man or woman. We can make a case out against any blooming one of 'em.' He at least had the decency to wait until Mrs Plum had left the room before setting out his solution to the problem fairly and squarely in front of his sergeant. 'Look,' he began, employing a wheedling tone which set MacGregor's teeth on edge, 'let's draw up a list and stick a pin in it eh? That way nobody can accuse us of unfair prejudice. We can easily juggle around with the evidence a bit so that it fits, and then we'll go and apply for a warrant. As soon as we've got the whole thing tied up nice and tight we'll call in the newspapers and the TV people. I'll hold a news conference and tell 'em all that I – Detective Chief Inspector Dover of New Scotland Yard – have solved this tricky murder case single-handed in less than twenty-bloody-hours. That'll hit the headlines – and make Pomeroy Chemicals sit up and take notice eh? Oh, that reminds me . . .' Dover came down from these dizzy heights and began rummaging aimlessly through his pockets. 'What the hell did I do with that bloody application form? You haven't nicked it have you, laddie?'

MacGregor said that no, he hadn't.

'Ah, got it! I knew I'd put it away safe somewhere.' Dover grinned happily and tucked the grubby little wad of paper back in his waistcoat pocket. 'I'll send it in as soon as we've got this bloody case cracked. 'Strewth, it couldn't have happened at a better time. A success like this and my name'll be a bloody household word!'

MacGregor sought to bring a touch of reality into the conversation by asking what would happen if they picked the wrong man.

'He'll get acquitted!' snarled Dover. ''Strewth, you tell me the last time one of mine didn't get acquitted! And he'll probably get compensation for false arrest or whatever it is. The last one bloody well did. Besides it won't matter then. I'll be on Pomeroy's payroll and' – Dover chuckled richly at the thought – 'they'll have to give me a golden handshake to get rid of me! Here, come to think of it, picking the wrong bleeding joker mightn't be a bad idea at that!' He was still mulling over this new plan for getting money without actually working for it as he licked the last smear of custard off his spoon. Then he turned to more important matters. 'Do you reckon she'd run to second helpings?' he asked MacGregor. 'Pop into the kitchen and tell her how good it was and ask if there's any more!'

But MacGregor qualified for the Victoria Cross and sat firm. We all have our breaking point and MacGregor's had just arrived. Over the years he had put up with a lot from Dover, but to be asked to subject an innocent man to the indignity of being tried for murder just so that Dover could land a cushy job with a commercial firm was too much. MacGregor took his courage in both hands and blurted out his declaration of independence. 'No!'

Dover had a full stomach and this kept his reaction down to a flicker of mild surprise. 'Why not? She won't eat you, laddie. She'll take it as a compliment to her cooking.'

MacGregor fought for self-control. No doubt the best thing would have been for him to have flung himself across the table and regardless of personal hygiene fastened his hands very tightly round Dover's unlovely throat. But MacGregor was still a policeman. He still retained that inculcated respect for his superiors which is proof against all the evidence of the senses. 'I was talking about framing one of the suspects actually, sir,' he said weakly.

'Oh?' Dover seemed puzzled. 'Well, see if you can get me another plateful of pud and we'll discuss it, eh? I mean' – Dover could have doubled as the embodiment of Sweet Reason – 'I'm easy. If there's somebody you'd like to fix – that's fine. I just suggested sticking a pin in the list for the hell of it. I don't give a monkey's which one of 'em we nab. And don't you start getting into a muck sweat about him giving us the slip on some blooming technicality. I haven't seen the joker yet that I couldn't bash a free and voluntary confession out of and not leave a mark on him – given a sound-proof cell, of course, and no witnesses and a bit of time. You just tell me which one, laddie, and I guarantee to bring him to trial at the very least and – who knows? – we might even get a conviction.' Benevolence could go no further. Dover beamed in an almost paternal manner at his sergeant before his face hardened slightly. 'Now, you nip along, laddie, and see about my second helping before that old cow scoffs the lot herself!'

To his eternal shame, MacGregor nipped. On his way back he called in at the public bar for a shot of Dutch courage and two pints of best bitter when he found Inspector Walters already there, carefully setting out three glasses of brandy on a small tray.

'Hello, sergeant!' he said in companionable greeting. 'I was just on my way to have a word with you and your governor.' He nodded his head at the glasses of brandy. 'I thought I'd push the boat out a bit, just to celebrate your first full day's work.'

MacGregor smiled feebly and, abandoning his own order for drinks, bought a couple of packets of cigarettes instead. They were, of course, Dover's favourite brand only in the sense that any brand paid for by somebody else was Dover's favourite.

'There's been a development,' said Inspector Walters as he pocketed his change. He indicated the folder he had tucked under his arm. 'I don't know if it'll lead to anything, but it's the first bit of bloody movement we've had in this case. I thought I'd better bring it round because your governor doesn't seem much of a one for going by the book, does he? Why, as far as I can tell, he's not so much as put his nose inside our Murder Headquarters since he got here.'

'Chief Inspector Dover has a very individual style of working,' agreed MacGregor, sticking conscientiously to the literal truth. 'Shall I take the tray for you, sir?' He would dearly have loved to ask Inspector Walters what the new development was, but the comparatively crowded bar was not the place for such confidences.

Inspector Walters failed to match MacGregor in tact and general delicacy of feeling. He went ahead to open the door which led out to the dining room and paused with his hand on the handle. 'I say,' he bawled back across the room, 'is it true that the young Bones kid had a piss in your governor's bowler hat?'

MacGregor scorned to answer so impertinent a question.

Dover had already eaten his second helping of pudding and was half-way through MacGregor's on the indisputable grounds that it would otherwise grow cold and go to waste. He was pleased to see the brandy, though less ecstatic about the arrival of Inspector Walters.

'A new development?' he whined. ''Strewth, couldn't it have waited till morning? I'm only flesh and blood, you know. I can't keep going twenty-four hours a day, seven days a week. I'm not made of iron. You should see the state of my bowels. I don't know whether it's overwork or the water in this dump or what, but ...'

'I was just telling Inspector Walters that we've already made considerable progress, sir,' said MacGregor, who knew that not everybody could take Dover's intestinal complications in their stride.

Dover scowled. 'I'm confidently expecting to make an arrest at any minute,' he announced. It was a phrase he'd picked up from those very old films on the telly.

Inspector Walters evinced some surprise. 'But you don't even know who the dead girl is yet, do you, sir?'

'That doesn't stop me from spotting the blooming murderer!' retorted Dover crossly. 'And have you checked up yet to see whether any of the people living in The Grove's got a criminal record?'

Inspector Walters was taken aback. 'You didn't ask me to, sir.'

Dover shrugged his shoulders. 'Thought you'd do it automatically,' he said, chalking this one up to himself.

Inspector Walters gulped and avoided MacGregor's eye. He was a man of some professional pride who didn't care to be found wanting. 'I'll get on to it right away, sir,' he promised.

'Suit yourself!' Dover sat back and allowed MacGregor to ply him with a cigarette. Having re-established the pecking order, the Chief Inspector felt he could afford to relax. 'So, what's this new stuff you're supposed to have come up with?' he asked.

Inspector Walters opened his folder. 'The forensic people from the lab came across it, sir. I don't know whether you could really call it a clue to the girl's identity, but it's the nearest we've had so far.'

9

'Of course,' said Inspector Walters, painfully conscious that his revelation had been something of an anti-climax, 'we've still got the option of putting the girl's photo on the telly. We'll get every crank in the country ringing up but ...'

'It's a bloody paper bag!' said Dover, indignantly and accusingly.

'Yes, sir.' Inspector Walters was beginning to wish he'd let one of his underlings bring the damned thing round and collect the glory. 'The forensic people have had quite a time with it, as you can see. It's disintegrated pretty badly. That's why they've put it between these two sheets of transparent plastic, sir, so that it doesn't crumble away any more. Still, you can read the writing on it quite clearly, can't you?'

Dover took hold of the talc and paper sandwich again and screwed his eyes up. The paper bag was a white one, some eight inches square, and it had obviously been folded up half a dozen times. It was a special bag, individually printed for the establishment concerned. 'Ermengilda's Kitchen', Dover read aloud in a voice of total disbelief. 'Gifte Shoppe & Café. Souvenirs. Home-made gâteaux a Speciality. Barford-in-the-Meadow.' He handed the sandwich to MacGregor and addressed himself to Inspector Walters. 'And what the hell am I supposed to do with that?'

Inspector Walters was so unnerved by this display of unashamed hostility that the obvious answer to Dover's question never so much as crossed his mind. 'I thought – we thought – it might narrow the search down, sir,' he bleated. 'Starting from Barford-in-the-Meadow, you see, and then widening out in ever increasing circles.'

'I'll give you ever increasing circles!' threatened Dover.

It was left to MacGregor to find some more constructive line of enquiry. 'Where precisely did they find this paper bag?'

Inspector Walters responded with touching gratitude. The relief of hearing a human voice! 'It was in her shoe, sergeant.'

'Her shoe?'

'Yes, she'd got a hole in the sole of her left shoe and this paper bag had been folded up and placed in the shoe, evidently in an attempt to keep the wet out. All her clothing was cheap, rubbishy stuff. Tatty. Her shoes were the same. I doubt if they would have stood up to re-soling, even supposing she'd got the money to pay for it. The lab people have been going through all her clothing with a fine tooth-comb in an effort to track down where she hailed from. It was all chain-store stuff. The sort you can buy in any one of a couple of hundred towns. It was pure chance, really, that one of the team thought of having a look at the soles of her shoes. They were looking more for particles of coal dust or sand or cement or something. The shoes had dried out a bit by then and he realized that there'd been this amateurish attempt to repair them. And that's how they found the paper bag.'

Inspector Walter's account tailed off lamely as Dover produced, without benefit of decently concealing hand, one of his enormous, jaw-cracking yawns. It was an awesome spectacle and, in its time, had put better men than Inspector Walters off their stride.

'And you think we might be able to trace the girl back through this?' MacGregor was merely ruminating aloud. The day had not yet dawned when he would seek advice from a provincial copper, however worthy.

Inspector Walters nodded. 'It's the only clue we've got.'

MacGregor was well aware of that. 'Barford-in-the-Meadow is quite a little tourist centre,' he pointed out. 'And a half-way stop for the long distance coaches. I can't see anybody at Ermengilda's Kitchen remembering a casual customer.'

'If she was a bloody customer at all,' contributed Dover, running a stubby finger round the inside of his glass and then licking off the very last traces of brandy. 'She could have picked that bag up in the street somewhere.'

'That's true, sir,' agreed MacGregor. He wouldn't have picked a paper bag up in the street himself, but he appreciated that not everyone would be so particular. 'And from what little we know about the girl, it does seem rather unlikely that she would be making purchases in a place like Ermengilda's Kitchen.' He tapped the plastic sandwich with an authoritative finger. 'These tourist-trap places are generally on the expensive side.'

'Doesn't that make it more likely that they would remember her, if she had been a customer?' asked Inspector Walters, and got two very bleak scowls for his pains.

Meanwhile, Dover, too, had been thinking. He was getting very bored with Frenchy Botham and a nice little run out into the country wouldn't come at all amiss. Especially one at the taxpayer's expense. They could have lunch at Barford-in-the-Meadow, ask a few questions and be back at The Laughing Dog in plenty of time for supper. A few hours' delay in reaching a final solution wouldn't worry Pomeroy Chemicals Limited all that much, and they'd be highly unlikely ever to find out the reason why. Dover felt almost happy and, since he was clearly going to put himself out on Inspector Walters's behalf, he considered he was fully justified in inviting that lucky man to stand another round of drinks. 'One,' he said with a winning leer, 'for the road, eh?'

Inspector Walters gathered up the empties.

Dover vouchsafed a final suggestion. 'How about making 'em doubles this time?'

If there were any justice in the world, Dover's day trip to Barford-in-the-Meadow would have been accomplished in either a thick fog or a blinding snowstorm. The day broke, however, bright and sunny and, although it was some hours before Dover got out of bed, the weather continued to be really rather superb. He and MacGregor had a most enjoyable drive in the police car which, in accordance with Dover's instructions, progressed slowly so that they could enjoy the burgeoning beauties of the English countryside.

All in all, it made a very nice break – a pleasant little interlude in the hard, unrelenting and exhausting grind of a murder investigation. They stopped for coffee and biscuits at The Caltraps in Lesser Wibbley, beer and crisps at The William & Mary in Horwill, and reached Barford-in-the-Meadow in time for an early lunch.

At three o'clock, when the bar closed, MacGregor managed to get Dover out of The Ploughboy's Arms and staggering once more along the path of duty. Having sensibly found out the location of Ermengilda's Kitchen while Dover was regaling the drinking public in the Snug with tales of his derring do, MacGregor was able to steer their steps past all the Ingle-nooks, the Copper Warming Pans and Delicatessens, and the Olde Patisserie Stores with which Barford-in-the-Meadow swarmed.

Ermengilda's Kitchen (Gifte Shoppe & Café) was an aggressive pastiche of what a middle-European set designer for an American film might have thought an eighteenth-century English coffee-house looked like. It was so quaint that it hurt. The windows were archly bowed and one in five of the little panes of glass was carefully distorted. The Kitchen was entered through an old-fashioned glass door which rang an old-fashioned bell – thus giving notice of the approach of yet another well-heeled sucker. It might have been better if the warning about the step had been printed in something more legible than olde English black letter, but MacGregor picked himself up in a jiffy and no great harm was done.

Miss Ermengilda herself came hurrying across as soon as she realized she wasn't going to be sued for damages. She was wearing buckled shoes, white stockings, a dirndl skirt, an embroidered blouse and a mob cap. 'Oh, dear, are you all right?'

MacGregor said that he was and tried to fend Miss Ermengilda off. In spite of the wholesome impression she gave of lavender bags and three-legged milking stools, her hands seemed to be everywhere.

'Wouldn't you care to sit down for just a moment or two? We have a chair over here ...'

She was too late, of course. The chair in question was already buckling under the seventeen and a quarter stones of solid fat of You-know-who.

'Oh!' squeaked Miss Ermengilda who prided herself on being patronized by such a very nice type of clientele.

Dover's wits were too scattered to allow much in the way of finesse. 'We're from the police,' he said, waving an arm which nearly swept every jar of Old-fashioned Humbugs right off the counter. 'I'm Detective Chief Inspector Dover and this is Detective Sergeant What's-his-name. 'Strewth, show her your warrant card, laddie, before she starts shouting rape!'

Several of the customers who had been happily ' just looking' began to leave.

'Is there perhaps somewhere we could have a few words in private, madam?' asked MacGregor, rightly judging that Miss Ermengilda was not best pleased at seeing her living slink out of the door.

Miss Ermengilda gazed round. Having the police on the premises had quite taken her breath away. 'Well, I suppose we could go ...'

'How about over there?' Dover launched himself off his chair by the counter and made it right across to the other end of the shop in an untidy scramble. As usual his instinct was infallible and he flopped down at one of the little café tables with a grunt of pure relief. His feet, after all that walking, were just about killing him. Indeed, had he been a little less squiffy, he would probably have taken his boots off to ease them.

After only a momentary hesitation to reconstitute the display of corn dollies which Dover's uncertain passage had casually demolished, Miss Ermengilda joined him. MacGregor brought up the rear.

'Doris!' Miss Ermengilda summoned a bored-looking teenager who was sketchily arrayed as a Victorian tweenie. 'Go and serve in the shop until I'm free, dear! And try and push that dried mimosa, there's a good girl! I can't face having it hanging around for another year.' Miss Ermengilda waited until Doris had gone on her way in a flurry of indifference. 'Now – er – gentlemen, what can I do for you?'

'How about a pot of tea for two and a plate of cakes?' asked Dover hopefully.

'Later, perhaps.' Miss Ermengilda was nobody's fool where business was concerned. She turned now to MacGregor, slightly disappointed that so nice looking a young man should have sunk so low.

MacGregor produced the paper bag from his brief-case. It was still being preserved between the two sheets of plastic and Miss Ermengilda regarded it dubiously. 'Did this paper bag come from your shop, madam?'

'I imagine so. Why do you want to know?'

'It's in connection with some enquiries we're making,' said MacGregor and waited patiently while Miss Ermengilda removed the bowl of lump sugar to a neighbouring table where it was out of reach of Dover's thieving fingers. 'Can you by any chance remember if you have ever seen this girl before?'

Miss Ermengilda accepted the proffered photograph. 'Good gracious,' she said faintly. 'Is she ... is she .. ?'

'Yes, I'm afraid she's dead, madam,' said MacGregor. 'It's her death, of course, which is the subject of our enquiries.'

Miss Ermengilda's throat had gone quite dry. 'Was she murdered?' she asked in a shocked voice.

MacGregor nodded his head.

'Good gracious!'

'Do you recall ever having seen her before?'

'Well, of course I do!' said Miss Ermengilda rather tartly as she handed the photograph back. 'It's Pearl, isn't it?'

MacGregor whipped notebook and pencil out with a speed of hand which deceived the eye. 'Pearl?' he repeated eagerly. 'Pearl who?'

'Pearl Wallace, of course. She worked for me until recently. Here in the café mostly, but helping out in the shop as and when required. I make a point of that, you know. Flexibility. They must be prepared to do both jobs, otherwise they stand around half the day doing absolutely nothing. These girls will *stand*, of course, until the cows come home.'

But MacGregor was after hard facts, not Miss Ermengilda's views on the mobility of adolescent female labour. And, all credit to Miss Ermengilda who was a much tougher cookie than she looked, facts were what he got.

Pearl Wallace was an eighteen-year-old who had graced Ermengilda's Kitchen with her presence for the best part of twelve months.

'Where did she live?'

'She was in lodgings. Jubilee Avenue. Number Eleven. Mrs O'Malley.'

'She didn't live at home?'

'No, she'd left home. I presumed that there'd been one of the usual teenage revolts. Pearl wasn't a very articulate girl, and in any case I make a point of never prying. One's motives are so liable to be misunderstood.'

'Do you know if she'd got a boyfriend?'

'I'm afraid I haven't the least idea. I expect she had. She was quite a pretty girl in a gamin sort of way.'

MacGregor tapped his teeth with the end of his pencil. They'd struck gold here, all right! At last! And it was all thanks to old Dover, would-you-believe! MacGregor spared a glance for the man responsible for this dramatic break-through. There he was – eyes shut, mouth open, chins sunk on his manly bosom – but still dominating the proceedings. MacGregor tore his eyes away from the sickening spectacle and went back to Miss Ermengilda. 'Did Pearl Wallace have any family?'

'Oh, I think there were some parents, if that's what you mean.'

'Do you know where they live?'

Miss Ermengilda shook her head. 'I imagine it's somewhere near Mottrell. That's where Pearl went to school. Mottrell Comprehensive. I know that because she gave the Headmaster as her reference when she came here.'

'And you took it up?'

'I certainly did!' said Miss Ermengilda bitterly. 'I've been let down too often by girls with simply glowing references to waste my time with those who can't produce any at all.'

'What sort of a worker was Pearl Wallace?'

Miss Ermengilda inclined her head judiciously. 'Average,' she said after a moment's thought. 'By which I mean she did as little work as possible, was completely uninterested in the job, and was not unduly scrupulous in money matters if she thought she could get away with it. On the other hand, she was quite personable and she kept herself clean. I wish I could say as much about all the girls who have been employed here. And now, sergeant' – Miss Ermengilda fixed MacGregor with a steely eye – 'I think it's time you told me a little more about what's happened.'

'Pearl Wallace is apparently the unknown girl whose dead body was found the other day in Frenchy Botham.'

Miss Ermengilda nodded. 'I remember reading about it in the paper. What on earth was she doing down there?'

'That's what we're trying to find out,' said MacGregor. 'You don't, if I may say so, seem very surprised at what's happened.'

Miss Ermengilda was craning her neck to see what was going on in the shop. 'Oh, I'm not,' she admitted frankly. 'Pearl Wallace was what I call one of Nature's victims. Some people seem to attract bad luck, don't they?'

'When did you last see her?'

Miss Ermengilda closed her eyes for this calculation. 'That would be Friday, the seventh of this month. She waited until after we'd finished serving the luncheons and then calmly informed me that she wouldn't be in at all the next day – which was a Saturday, if you please. The busiest day of the week! I was simply furious and I said so. She answered me very pertly and so, really, I had no choice. I gave her a week's notice. She told me precisely what I could do with it, collected the wages due to her and her cards from my desk, and marched out. Naturally, I haven't seen her since then – nor, indeed, did I expect to.'

MacGregor glanced around. 'Was she particularly friendly with any of your other staff?'

Wordlessly Miss Ermengilda indicated the fair Doris who was casually assuring an anxious American lady that, if she wanted to take some real English candy back to the States with her, she couldn't do better than a nice box of Edinburgh rock.

'We'd better have a word with her, I suppose,' said Mac-Gregor, already feeling in his bones that they weren't going to get much enlightenment from Doris.

'I'll send her over!' offered Miss Ermengilda quickly. She was itching to get her hands on that American woman.

MacGregor gestured vaguely in the direction of the comatose Dover. 'Perhaps we could have some tea at the same time?'

'I should have thought a pot of strong black coffee would have been more to the point,' observed Miss Ermengilda with a sniff. Then she realized that this couple of time-wasting policemen were tranforming themselves into a couple of paying customers. 'Tea for two and cakes? I'll give the order myself. Oh, by the way' – she paused as the query struck her – 'what was Pearl Wallace doing with one of our paper bags?'

'She was using it to patch a hole in one of her shoes.'

Miss Ermengilda's lips clamped together in a hard line. 'And that,' she informed MacGregor grimly, 'is where one's profits go! Oh, these dratted girls!'

It was over ten minutes before Doris and the afternoon tea arrived. Dover, rousing on the instant like an old war horse hearing the bugles, showed no surprise at finding a young lady in fancy dress sharing the table with him. He contented himself with reaching across for the plate of Olde Danish pastries.

Doris herself had undergone something of a metamorphosis. Ermengilda's Kitchen didn't sport all that many handsome young men amongst its patrons, and Doris had no intention of wasting the opportunity. During her brief sojourn in the kitchen, she had wielded mascara, eye-shadow, hair spray, lipstick and cheap scent with a liberal hand.

For once in his life MacGregor was almost pleased that he'd got Dover with him.

10

When it came down to brass tacks, however, Doris wasn't all that helpful. 'Well, I knew Pearl, natch,' she said, pulling out her pocket mirror and examining her face intently in it. 'She sort of taught me the job when I first come here, didn't she?' She poked out a finger and began to rub the lipstick off her teeth. 'I've only been here a couple of months, see? Actually, I'm thinking of jacking it in. It's dead boring, you know. I might try and get a job abroad. Like on the Coster Bravo or the South of France. Pearl? Oh, yes ... well, I sort of only knew her in the shop, you know. We didn't go out together or anything. I did ask her round to our house once, but my mum didn't take to her. Thought she was sort of sly. Well, she did sort of keep herself to herself, if you see what I mean. My mum didn't go much on Pearl living in lodgings, either. Said it wasn't natural for a girl of her age. Said no good would come of it. And she was right, wasn't she?'

For reasons best known to himself, Dover decided to take a hand in the interrogation. He was probably trying to speed things up as he was finding Doris's shrill and adenoidal voice very wearing on the ear. 'Did you know she was pregnant?'

'Pearl?' Doris's cup of excitement was filled to over-flowing. 'Pregnant? Go on!' Her eyes glinted and she nodded her head in a knowing manner. 'Well, I can't say as how I'm surprised, really. She never said nothing, of course, but I had wondered. She sort of kept looking at herself in mirrors and things, to see if anything was showing. She'd got very short tempered, too. Some days you couldn't say nothing to her without her flaring up, like, and jumping right down your throat. She'd got very sort of bitter, too.'

'About men?' asked MacGregor.

'About everybody,' said Doris, lowering her eyelids seductively. 'Kept saying things like she was fed up with always being a door mat and that it was about time somebody else footed the bill for a change.'

Dover waited a moment in case Doris was going to elaborate on this statement. She wasn't. 'What did she mean?'

'Search me.'

'You didn't ask?'

'What for? I've got my own troubles, haven't I?'

MacGregor consulted his notebook for inspiration. 'Do you know anything about her boyfriends? Was there anybody special?'

'I dunno. She used to hang around with some of them lads from the big RAF camp down the road. I reckon that's why she hung on here for so long. Well, it's not everywhere that's got a supply of boys like that on tap, is it? 'Course, they're only Erks, but even so.' Doris tossed her head and rearranged her hair on her shoulders. 'You won't catch me hanging round a dump like this when I leave home,' she said. 'I'll be off to London. Or New York. Or somewhere.'

'Why did she ask for the day off on the Saturday, the day before she got the sack?'

'Search me.' Doris was beginning to get bored. Had the conversation centred round her she might have displayed more animation. But—about a mere fellow worker and a dead one at that? Dullsville!

It was Dover who succeeded in getting her to adopt a more helpful attitude. Nubile young women had long since ceased to have any effect upon his blood pressure and this enabled him to take a less indulgent line. He addressed MacGregor across Doris.

'Let's take her down to the nick,' he said. 'Her memory might improve after a few hours shut up all alone in a rat-infested police cell.'

'Ooh, you wouldn't dare!' squealed Doris.

Dover leered. 'Wouldn't I?'

'Well, I'm doing my best, honest.' Doris pouted prettily and edged nearer to MacGregor.

'They can send you to prison for it.'

Doris, wide-eyed, stared at Dover. 'For what?'

'For withholding information from the police in the execution of their bloody duty,' explained Dover, managing to make it sound like a hanging job.

'Aw, come off it!' Doris giggled as she remembered that you didn't have to bother about Authority or policemen or anything, really, in these enlightened days.

'You'll see!' promised Dover menacingly.

Doris relaxed completely and produced the clincher. 'My dad's a shop steward!' she announced gleefully. 'You try pushing me around, copper, and you'll have a general strike on your hands!'

Dover scowled but, in view of his imminent entry into the world of industry via Pomeroy Chemicals Limited, he decided not to take any risks. The last thing he wanted at that particular moment in time was to find himself in the middle of some sordid trade union dispute. He contented himself with shoving his cup across for a refill and allowed the business of incarcerating the fair Doris in a dungeon to drop.

MacGregor poured the oil. 'It's just that we were counting on you being able to help us,' he told Doris with a sad little smile. 'Pearl was a friend of yours, you know, and somebody did kill her. Can't you think of anything that might help us?'

Doris played with the sugar bowl. 'Well, there was that telephone call,' she said grudgingly.

MacGregor tried not to pounce. 'She got a telephone call?'

'No, dumbie, she made one! Here, don't go telling old Ermengilda, will you? She'd go spare if she knew we was using her phone for private calls.'

MacGregor promised, being more concerned with murder than ethics. 'When did she make this call?'

'Oh, the Monday or the Tuesday before she cleared off. Or it might have been the Wednesday. One day's much the same as another in this lousy dump.'

'And who did she make it to?'

Doris looked surprised. 'Well, I don't know, do I? I was outside the office keeping guard in case old Ermengilda come sneaking back, wasn't I? All I know is she wanted a Birmingham number.'

'A Birmingham number?' MacGregor's noble brow crinkled up as he tried to make head or tail of this new piece of information.

''Sright.' Doris was busy examining her finger-nails. 'We couldn't find that little book with the dialling codes in it, could we? So she had to ring 'em up and ask what it was. That's how I come to know it was Birmingham she wanted.'

'But you don't know the number?'

''Course I don't, stupid!' Doris was no longer finding MacGregor very attractive. He was quite good looking, of course, but – oh, Dragsville! 'Once she got the code, she dialled the number, didn't she? What was I supposed to do? Count the clicks?'

MacGregor glanced hopefully at Dover on the off chance that he might be preparing to lash out again. Pity. MacGregor would have quite liked to see Doris get a thumping.

'And,' concluded Doris, pushing her chair back and standing up, 'I didn't hear what Pearl said because I was outside the room with the door closed. Added to which, I wasn't blooming well interested. Can I go now? Miss Ermengilda's been looking daggers at me for ages and I don't want to get into her bad books just along of you lot, do I?'

MacGregor slipped in a final question as Miss Ermengilda bore down on them. 'Do you know of anybody who'd be likely to want to murder Pearl Wallace?'

Doris hadn't the least. Nor had Miss Ermengilda, to whom MacGregor posed the same query.

Miss Ermengilda managed the distressing business of grossly over-charging her customers with considerable aplomb and then enquired if the case was likely to generate any publicity.

'It might,' said MacGregor, counting his change unbelievingly for the second time. 'There's not been much so far, but the media may start taking an interest now that we've got a name for the victim.'

Miss Ermengilda was writhing genteelly on the horns of a dilemma. 'Of course, publicity is very welcome,' she admitted, 'but it must be the right kind, mustn't it? One wouldn't like Ermengilda's Kitchen to be mixed up in anything distasteful.' She broke off as Dover tugged rather urgently at her arm.

'Got a bog here, missus?'

Miss Ermengilda tried, and failed, to disengage herself. 'I beg your pardon!'

'A wc,' said Dover, giving his victim a shake. 'A privy! A loo! The jakes!'

'He means a gentlemen's cloakroom,' explained MacGregor, wondering why Dover, who was not normally mealy-mouthed, couldn't call a spade a spade.

'I'm afraid not,' murmured Miss Ermengilda faintly. She was still attempting to unhook Dover's sausage-thick fingers from her arm. 'You'll have to use the public convenience.'

'Where is it?'

'In the square outside. Just behind the Jubilee Oak.'

Dover was already on the move. 'That a pub?'

Miss Ermengilda was glad for once that there were so few customers in her establishment. 'No!' she hissed. 'It's a tree, planted to commemorate Queen Victoria's Golden Jubilee and one of our main tourist attractions.'

Dover was at the shop door before it occurred to him that his abrupt departure required some explanation. 'Shan't be a tick!' he called back to MacGregor. 'It must be those bloody salts I took last night.'

In normal circumstances, of course, one would not dream of penetrating behind doors that ought to remain for ever closed to one but, on this particular occasion, an incident took place which, although of an intimate nature, did have some slight bearing on Chief Inspector Dover's future conduct of the case.

A time came when, not to put too fine a point on it, Dover was in urgent need of paper. The supplies provided by the local Sanitary Department had been exhausted some time ago, and Dover was reduced to searching through his pockets. He could find only one piece that was of an acceptable size and texture: the application form for the position of Chief Security Officer with Pomeroy Chemicals Limited. There was a moment's hesitation, but only a moment's. Dover was never the man to get his priorities wrong and, anyhow, he could always send off for another application form.

But, somehow, even at that moment, he knew that he wasn't going to bother. There is a lot to be said for Public Service, especially for the bone idle. The stresses and strains, the cut and thrust of commercial life – these, Dover realized, were not for him. With one firm pull, he despatched both Ambition and the application form. Then, feeling happier and more at ease with himself than he had done for some time, he adjusted his clothing before leaving, and left.

MacGregor was waiting for him outside with the police car.

''Strewth, that's better!' sighed Dover, sinking thankfully down on the back seat. 'You don't think she could have put something in that tea, do you? Here' – the car had started moving as soon as MacGregor had shut his door – 'where are we going?'

'To the house Pearl Wallace lodged in, sir. Her landlady should be able to give us the girl's home address and, with any luck, a great deal more information about her, too.'

'Pearl Wallace?'

MacGregor blamed himself, really. He, if anybody, should have remembered that Dover needed treating like the mental deficient he was. 'The dead girl, sir.'

'I know, I know!' snapped Dover, having had time to work it out for himself. 'What about that RAF station?'

MacGregor nodded. 'You think that the putative father might possibly be an airman, sir? Yes, that idea had crossed my mind.

The only trouble is that there are something like a thousand men on that station and they're always changing. An investigation there would involve us in an awful lot of work and I was wondering if we mightn't just leave it for the moment until we've something more to go on. Perhaps later on . . .'

'Good idea!' said Dover who would have postponed everything to the morrow, if he could. 'Besides, we've already decided that the real dad's sitting on his backside in Frenchy Botham.'

'That's only a theory, sir,' warned MacGregor. 'We must try to keep an open mind.'

'I'd be happy,' said Dover, suddenly mindful of his troubles, 'if I could just keep an open bowel.'

Mrs O'Malley was not unaccustomed to finding policemen on her doorstep though it was the first time she'd encountered Scotland Yard. She thoughtfully examined her visitors' credentials before making her own position crystal clear. She was a poor widow woman who scratched a meagre living by letting off a few furnished rooms on a weekly basis. Not being blessed by much in the way of book learning, Mrs O'Malley ran a strictly cash-in-advance business. No cheques, no credit cards, no credit.

'And that's the only interest I take in my tenants,' she said, folding thin arms over a thin bosom. 'I don't mother 'em and I don't pry into their affairs and I don't give 'em advice. I just stand here every Friday night and hold my hand out. If they haven't got it, they don't stay. I've got a son in the next street. He takes after his father. Six foot two in his stocking feet, shoulders like an ox and a nasty temper to go with it. I don't ' – she allowed the faintest hint of a smile to play on the uncompromising line of her lips – 'usually have any trouble.'

MacGregor pointed out that Pearl Wallace had been missing for nearly a fortnight.

Mrs O'Malley agreed, without any sign of involvement whatsoever, that this was so. 'She paid me on the seventh and I kept the room for her till the fifteenth. A couple of days later this blackie turns up. Well, his money's as good as anybody else's. I let him have the room.'

MacGregor sighed. 'You didn't think of informing the police that the girl was missing?'

'You get no thanks for it.'

'What did you do with her things?'

'Cleared 'em out. Not that there was all that much. Just a few clothes and bits and pieces that wouldn't fetch half a dollar if you was to try and sell 'em.'

'You didn't throw them away?' asked MacGregor.

Mrs O'Malley indignantly drew herself up to her full height. 'I should think I didn't! I packed 'em away in a cardboard box and I've got it in my room. Do you want to see it?'

'We may have to take it away,' said MacGregor as he and Dover followed Mrs O'Malley downstairs into the basement where she had her own bed-sitting room.

The television was on and Mrs O'Malley, having deposited the cardboard box on the table, made no move to switch it off. 'I'll be glad to see the back of it,' she announced as she settled herself down in her chair again to watch the second half of Crossroads. 'I'll want a receipt, of course.'

The cardboard box yielded precisely nothing. It merely confirmed the almost ephemeral nature of Pearl Wallace's life. A few cheap, mass-produced garments, one or two items of inexpensive make-up, a couple of tawdry teenage magazines. No letters.

Mrs O'Malley, her eyes riveted to the screen, was as helpful as ever. 'How should I know? I sort out my own letters and dump the rest on the table in the hall. I can't remember whether she got any letters or not. No, now I tell a lie! She did get one, not long before she scarpered. One of those official ones in a long brown envelope. Typed. At least' – Mrs O'Malley calmly proceeded to dash every hope in sight – 'I think it was for her, but I could be mistaken.'

MacGregor asked if he might see the room which Pearl Wallace had occupied and Mrs O'Malley, making it very clear that this ranked as an Imposition, consented. 'It'll do you no good,' she forecast as she took down her bunch of duplicate keys from a nail. 'I gave that room a right good clean out when I re-let it. You'll not find any of your clues there now.'

MacGregor opened the door for her. 'Even so . . .'

Mrs O'Malley pushed past. 'I'll tell you one thing, though,' she said as she started laboriously up the stairs. 'You might let me have her key back sometime. Look, it'll be a Yale one like this . . .'

Dover indulged himself in a little belch and then, taking Mrs O'Malley's chair, settled down to see what cosy catastrophes Meg Mortimer was coping with this week.

And so another day of unremitting toil came to an end. All in all, MacGregor reckoned that they'd made some progress. They had found out the dead girl's name, where she worked and where she lived. And all this had been achieved without Dover unearthing a single new murder suspect. He'd tried, of course, but it had been very half-hearted. Even he hadn't quite been able to see any of the Barford-in-the-Meadow lot following Pearl Wallace all the way to Frenchy Botham and there killing her.

'I didn't go much on that landlady woman,' said Dover as, sitting well back, he filled the entire police car with cigarette smoke. 'You'd have thought she'd have wondered where the girl was, wouldn't you?'

MacGregor was deep in speculation, trying to decide if Dover would notice if he wound down the window a crack. 'I'm afraid the truth is that nobody cared two hoots about Pearl Wallace, sir. And it's not only Mrs O'Malley and Ermengilda's Kitchen. What about the girl's family? Nobody's been making enquiries about her from that direction, either. Poor Pearl Wallace seems to have been a complete nonentity, doesn't she, sir?'

Dover stretched his legs out. 'They always lumber me with these crummy old cases,' he grumbled. 'Anything that hits the headlines, they keep for themselves.'

MacGregor tried to look on the bright side. 'Never mind, sir! I expect Pomeroy Chemicals can recognize a good professional job when they see it, whether it gets a lot of publicity or not.'

By now Dover had all but forgotten who the hell Pomeroy Chemicals were. 'D'you know,' he said, his eyes glazing over quite dreamily, 'I've always wanted to investigate a murder that had got somebody from the Royal Family mixed up in it. Either way,' he added generously. 'Victim or killer. 'Strewth, that'd get me in the history books, never mind the bloody newspapers! It'd get world coverage. I'd be able to write a book about it. Several books, probably. And then there'd be interviews and film rights and ...'

MacGregor waited to see if Dover was going to finish the sentence, but he wasn't. Even day-dreaming about work seemed to tire him out.

'Oh, well, sir,' said MacGregor, 'there's always tomorrow, isn't there?'

'Is there?'

'And, speaking of tomorrow, sir' – MacGregor thought he had made the transition really rather skilfully – 'I was thinking that we ought to go and see the Headmaster of Mottrell Comprehensive School. You remember, sir, he's the man who gave Pearl Wallace the reference that enabled her to get the job at Ermengilda's Kitchen.'

'What the hell do we want to see him for?'

'We've got to see anybody who can give us any information about Pearl Wallace, sir.'

Dover tipped his bowler hat down over his eyes and a few specks of rudely disturbed dandruff floated down onto the shoulders of his overcoat. ''Strewth!' he grunted disgustedly.

The Secretary of the Headmaster of Mottrell Comprehensive School was a woman of ample bosom and great calm. Christened 'The Forlorn Hope' by a member of the teaching staff who was more interested in military history than sex, she prided herself on taking everything in her stride. After nineteen gruelling years in the world of secondary education, the arrival of a couple of detectives from Scotland Yard didn't raise so much as a flicker.

'The Headmaster is expecting you,' she acknowledged. 'I'll let him know you've arrived.' She depressed the switch of the intercom on her desk. 'It's Miss Hope here, Headmaster!'

'Carmen Miranda!' crackled the intercom.

'Vladivostok!' responded Miss Hope placidly. She took time off to put her visitors in the picture. 'Today's password. That's to let him know that I'm not contacting him whilst under duress. If I'd been standing here with a knife at my throat, I should have said, "Little Dorrit".' She addressed the intercom again 'Detective Chief Inspector Dover from New Scotland Yard has arrived with his sergeant. Shall I show them in?'

The intercom croaked anxiously and unintelligibly.

Miss Hope permitted herself a slight gesture of impatience. 'Yes, I have examined their credentials, Headmaster, and no, they are not carrying offensive weapons of any kind.' She switched off and got to her feet. 'This way, gentlemen.'

Dover and MacGregor, intrigued but not in view of Miss Hope's supremely composed manner liking to comment, followed her obediently across the office to a communicating door largely labelled: 'PRIVATE! NO ENTRY!! KEEP OUT!!! THIS MEANS *YOU*!!!!'

Miss Hope raised a capable looking hand and knocked. Two loud knocks. A pause. Two soft knocks. Another pause. Three loud knocks in rapid succession.

There was a short wait and then came the sound of chains being rattled, keys being turned and bolts being withdrawn. The door opened and Miss Hope returned to her desk. Dover and MacGregor entered the inner sanctum.

'Do, please, sit down!' The Headmaster, having conscientiously re-chained, re-locked and re-bolted his door, blocked it for good measure with a heavy filing cabinet before scurrying back for cover behind his desk.

Dover regarded the two wooden chairs with some disapproval but, since that was all there was, he moved one nearer to the desk and prepared to deposit his weary bones on it. Or, at least, he tried to move it. Both chairs were, as it happens, securely bolted to the floor.

'A Senior Geography teacher in Crawley,' explained the Headmaster with a death's head grin, 'had his skull fractured the other day by an umbrella stand. One can't take too many precautions. Now' – nervously he realigned the pick-axe handle with the edge of his blotter – 'I understand you want some information about an ex-pupil of ours called Pearl Wallace?'

MacGregor took his eyes away from the windows which were well protected with fine-mesh chicken wire and tried to concentrate on the enquiries he was being paid to make. 'Do you recognize this girl, sir?'

The Headmaster cringed away instinctively as MacGregor got up to pass his photograph of the dead girl across the desk. 'No,' he said quickly, 'I don't.'

'But you've hardly looked at it, sir!' MacGregor spoke sharply.

'I don't have to, sergeant. I have nearly two thousand pupils in my care. They are continually changing and I've so managed things that nowadays I hardly ever see any of them. The whole art of being the head of a comprehensive school,' he added sententiously, 'is delegation. I have succeeded in delegating practically everything, except the over-all responsibility, of course, and the paperwork. What,' he asked as he wiped the palms of his hands on a large white handkerchief, 'is the point of having a staff of seventy if you don't trust them, eh?'

Dover was looking very boot-faced. He didn't relish the prospect of having to move again when he'd only just got settled. 'There must be somebody who can tell us about the bloody girl.'

The Headmaster winced visibly at the brusqueness of this remark. 'Oh, I have all the information here, all right,' he said, removing the cosh which he had been using as a paperweight and picking up a bright pink folder. 'This is Pearl Wallace's file. Everything we know about her is in here.'

Dover pouted discontentedly. He was allergic to paper. 'We were looking for more of the personal touch,' he grumbled. 'Like somebody who knew her and could fill us in about what sort of a kid she was.'

'Not a hope!' The Headmaster shook his head firmly. 'It's two years since she left and all her classroom contemporaries will have departed, too. And if there's one thing my teaching staff are it's *uninvolved*. It might be different if the girl had made her mark in some way or another. If she'd been very good or very bad. Those are the ones who tend to stick in the memory, however much one tries to forget them. But Pearl' – he looked at the cover of the folder for the surname – 'Pearl Wallace was nondescript to the point of vanishing, one might say. She was outstanding only in being perfectly average. Or' – he rifled professionally through the papers – 'just a little below average, if anything.'

'Could I have a look, sir?' MacGregor stretched out his hand slowly so as not to cause undue alarm and panic.

'Certainly not!' The Headmaster clutched the file possessively to his chest. 'These records are highly confidential.'

'We can easily get the necessary authorization, sir,' said Mac-Gregor in a bored voice. Past experience had taught him that such threats usually did the trick.

But the Headmaster of Mottrell Comprehensive was made of sterner stuff. He had not devoted twelve years of his life to these records for nothing. 'In that case, sergeant,' he responded loftily, 'I suggest you go ahead and get it. Until such time as you do, these documents do not leave my hands.'

It was Dover who found a way out of the impasse. 'Maybe you could read us out a few bits,' he said, more reasonably and more understandingly than was his wont, but still determined not to shift for at least the next half hour.

The Headmaster cautiously agreed that such a course of action might be possible. 'What sort of thing did you want to know? She got a prize for Scriptural Knowledge in her first year here, and she sprained a finger playing netball when she was in III(d). Not badly, I'm glad to say, as the injury was dealt with by our own Sick Bay.'

Dover slumped in his chair. 'What about boyfriends?' He glanced across at MacGregor and snapped his fingers. That was his charming way of indicating that he wanted a cigarette.

There was a moment of confusion as the Headmaster dived down behind his desk and it took MacGregor some time before he could make him understand that the sounds he had heard were not those of a high-powered rifle. Then there was the problem of settling Dover, whose own nerves were in no very steady state after all the commotion. The information that smoking was not permitted within those particular confines of Academe seemed likely to prove the last straw.

'Why the bloody hell not?'

An ashen-faced (and non-smoking) Headmaster stuck to his guns with the doggedness of which only the inherently timid are capable. 'It's a bad example for the children!' he bleated.

Dover snatched the matches out of MacGregor's hesitating hand and lit up defiantly. 'There aren't any bloody kids here!'

'There are bloody kids everywhere!' moaned the Headmaster, rocking desperately backwards and forwards in his chair. 'They're here all the time, watching and listening and sniffing. I try to keep them out but I'm fighting a losing battle. Dear God, don't you people outside realize that Pupil Power has already taken over. It's the hand that's still *in* the cradle that's rocking the world!'

'In that case,' snarled Dover, puffing smoke in all directions like the most satanic of those dark mills, 'a few more fags here or there won't make a ha'porth of bloody difference, will they?'

The three men remained closeted together for another hour without anything very profitable being achieved by anybody. This wasn't as big a waste of Public Money as might at first appear, as none of them had really anything better to do with their time. In the end Dover and MacGregor were forced to beat their retreat with nothing more than the last known address of the girl's parents to show for their morning's pains.

'And I'm telling you,' said Dover when they were back once again sharing the rear seat of the police car, 'that we'll go and see Mr and Mrs What-d'you-call-'em tomorrow.'

'But it seems such a waste of time, sir, to go all the way back to Frenchy Botham only to have to do the same journey again tomorrow. The Wallaces only live a mile or so away. We could be there in a matter of minutes.'

'And have to break the news to them that their blooming daughter's been croaked?' Dover's heavy jowls wobbled indignantly. ''Strewth, you know what it'll be like. We'll have 'em blubbering and snivelling all over the place. And we'd not get a sensible answer out of 'em for bloody hours. It'll be much better to let the local coppers handle it and us move in later when they're over the shock.'

'I doubt if there'll be all that much grief, sir,' observed MacGregor rather sadly. 'The girl's been missing for some time now and the parents seem to have done damn-all about it.'

Dover had found more arguments for his comfort. 'Identification!' he trumpeted, slapping a fat hand on an even fatter knee. 'One of 'em'll have to come down to Frenchy Botham to identify the body. We'll have 'em both shipped along tomorrow and then I can interview 'em in peace and quiet at my leisure.'

MacGregor was dismayed. 'But wouldn't it be better to see them against the background of their own environment, sir? I know Pearl Wallace wasn't living there at the time of her death, but it was presumably her home for the greater part of her life. You see, she seems to be such a nebulous sort of person, sir, that I feel any information we can get about her is valuable.'

'We're investigating a murder, laddie!' Dover reminded him with that special sneer he reserved for anything smacking of the intellectual, 'not doing an in-depth psychological study, for God's sake! Besides, if she was all that bloody wishy-washy, she wouldn't have gone and got herself killed, would she? She must have managed to get up somebody's nose.'

'Yes, and she managed to get herself pregnant, too, sir,' agreed MacGregor. 'I see your point. Poor kid, she didn't have much of a life.'

Dover was indignant. 'You want to save your sympathy for the living, laddie!' he snorted. 'There's some of us who have to keep soldiering on no matter what.'

In the end a compromise was reached. In return for yet another expensive hotel lunch (plus liquid refreshment) Dover agreed to visit the Wallaces in their own home that very afternoon, provided that somebody else had broken the tragic news to them first.

MacGregor installed Dover in the nearest bar and rushed off to make the necessary arrangements and cash another cheque.

By the time Dover and MacGregor loomed up on the scene, the Wallaces had got over their initial shock and were now in the mood to start looking for a scapegoat. Or, at least, Mrs Wallace was. Mr Wallace liked a quiet life, though he had of course found out quite early on that agreeing with Mrs Wallace was the surest way of getting it.

Mrs Wallace hardly waited until she'd got Dover and Mac-Gregor trapped in the three-piece suite in her front room. 'I think it's disgusting!' she complained, opening her innings with an impressive display of righteous indignation. 'A young girl like that! What were the police doing, that's what I'd like to know!'

'You've no doubt that the photograph you were shown is of your daughter, Pearl?'

Mrs Wallace fixed MacGregor with an angry glare and agreed that there was no doubt. 'And I recognized the description of her clothes.' She dabbed at her eyes. 'I bought her that pantie and bra set myself, for her birthday. No, it's our Pearl, all right. I knew something terrible would happen to her.'

Mr Wallace put his two-pennyworth in while his wife indulged herself noisily in her grief. 'They're taking us down there to-morrow to make the formal identification. We're both going to go. It should be a nice run if the rain keeps off.'

MacGregor kept an impassive face. 'When did your daughter leave home?'

'The minute she could!' snapped Mrs Wallace. 'She was just turned seventeen. Collected her birthday presents, got herself this job in Barford-in-the-Meadow and she was off. Just when we'd every right to expect a bit of a return on all the money we've laid out all these years. Why, we even let her spend a year at one of these commercial schools so's she could learn to be a secretary, though for all the good it did I don't know why we bothered. Paying, of course. She could have gone to the Tech but we were prepared to make sacrifices so that she could have the best.'

'You get nothing for nothing in this world,' said Mr Wallace, nodding his head wisely. 'I always say that.'

MacGregor remained looking at Mrs Wallace. 'Did your daughter give any reason for leaving home?'

'No. She just said she was going, and she went.'

'Was there anybody else involved? A man, for instance?'

Mrs Wallace bridled. 'Not as far as I know. Besides, our Pearl wasn't that sort of girl. She'd much rather watch television.'

'They told you that she was pregnant?'

'They told me,' agreed Mrs Wallace grimly, 'but I don't know as how I believed it.' It was a statement that seemed to put an effective stop to that line of questioning.

MacGregor plodded on, though. He clarified a few dates and settled the odd minor detail. Then there didn't seem to be much more he could do. Barring some really extraordinary development, the dead girl was definitely Pearl Wallace, only child of Mr and Mrs Wallace. She had left home and gone to work in Barford-in-the-Meadow as a waitress. About her recent history, her parents seemed to know even less than the police did. There hadn't been a complete break, though. Mrs Wallace acknowledged that they knew the girl's address and . . .

'There was the card for my birthday.'

Mr Wallace nodded his head again. 'And she rang up to wish us a Happy Christmas. She wasn't ungrateful. No, people can say what they like, but that girl wasn't ungrateful.'

Dover sank deeper into his chair. From not having wanted to come, he now as usual didn't want to go. Well, not yet. Not when he'd just got comfortable. He was annoyed to see that that idiot MacGregor appeared to be running out of questions.

Dover cleared his throat and both Mr and Mrs Wallace glanced instinctively upwards to see if that crack in the ceiling had suddenly got worse. Dover waited impatiently until their attention was focused back on him. Naturally he didn't like asking for afternoon tea just like that. This was a house of bereavement, after all. He cleared his throat once again and, unable to think of anything new, went trundling back over the same old ground. 'Are you sure she didn't have any reason for leaving home?'

Mrs Wallace expressed herself just as sure as she'd been the first time the question had been put.

Dover drew on his own extensive experience of family life. 'There wasn't a row or anything?'

'No!' Mrs Wallace wasn't having any of *that*, thank you very much!

Mr Wallace, on the other hand, was anxious to be helpful. 'Not a row, exactly,' he said. 'And not then, either, come to that.'

Dover blinked. 'And what the hell's that supposed to mean?'

Mr Wallace looked apprehensively at Mrs Wallace, and then he looked at Dover. For the first time in his life he realized what it was really like to be caught between the devil and the deep blue sea. He wasn't given time to work out the odds.

Dover who, during the entire course of this investigation,

hadn't yet been able to sink his fist into anybody's face began to make some ominous rumbles and actually looked as though he might leap aggressively to his feet at any moment.

Mr Wallace quickly, and erroneously, decided that Nell probably wasn't as cross as she looked.

'Well, if you ask me,' he said defensively, 'our Pearl was never the same since she found out she was adopted. It seemed to upset her somehow. She didn't say much but, if you ask me, things were never the same after that.'

12

Mr Wallace's revelation seemed to have released some inner spring in Mrs Wallace. In spite of Dover's unwillingness to act as an unpaid father confessor, he was more or less obliged to sit there while his hostess let it all come pouring out.

It appeared that Mr and Mrs Wallace, both veritable cat's cradles of complexes and inhibitions, had been unable to have children, and, faced with the fecundity of their numerous friends and relations, had been bitterly ashamed of their failure to contribute to the population explosion. When, after many trials and tribulations, they had managed to adopt a baby girl, they had broken off all connection with their respective families and former life, and moved right away from Edgbaston to start again from scratch in Mottrell.

'We made up our minds we were going to bring her up as our very own little girl,' explained Mrs Wallace, beginning to get weepy. 'That's what makes it all so awful now, you see. All that time and trouble and money and sacrifices, all wasted. Eighteen years of it and all gone for nothing, as you might say. Why, we could have had a car or holidays abroad or *anything*. Here' – she interrupted her lamentations to strike a more overtly practical note – 'what was she doing in this place she was killed in, anyway?'

'Frenchy Botham?' said MacGregor. 'We haven't been able to find out yet. We were hoping you might be able to tell us.'

Mrs Wallace shook her head. 'A village, is it? I've never heard of it.'

'Me neither,' said Mr Wallace.

Mrs Wallace resumed her story. 'We never told her she was adopted, you see,' she said as she folded and refolded the sodden handkerchief she was clutching. 'That's why we finished with all our relations. One of 'em would have been sure to blab it all out sooner or later, and neither me nor Mr Wallace was going to have the finger of shame pointed at our little Pearl.'

MacGregor was doing his best to follow Mrs Wallace's saga on the off-chance that she might say something useful. Occasionally, however, even he got lost. 'Finger of shame, Mrs Wallace? I don't quite understand.'

Mrs Wallace glanced furtively round her own over-crowded sitting room and lowered her voice to a barely audible whisper. 'Well, she was one of those, wasn't she? Illegit. I mean, they don't tell you much but they did tell us that. You know – her mother wasn't – well – married.'

'She didn't even know who the father was,' added Mr Wallace morosely before being silenced by a warning glare from his wife.

'We weren't,' declared Mrs Wallace with noble simplicity, 'going to have our little chick called a bastard.'

It was MacGregor who broke into the ensuing respectful silence. He could see that Dover was wilting and he always felt it made such a bad impression when a senior, top-ranking Scotland Yard officer just got up and walked out in the middle of somebody else's sentence. 'Er – how did your daughter find out she was an adopted child?'

Well, it was a long and complicated story which not even MacGregor thought was worth the trouble of unravelling. It was something to do with passports and a school trip to Holland, and MacGregor was content to let it go at that.

'I was so took aback,' declared Mrs Wallace, 'when she asked me that I couldn't think of anything to say. So I just told her the truth. That did it, of course. She took it very hard. Almost overnight she seemed to sort of turn right against us.'

'I reckon she'd always half suspected it,' said Mr Wallace.

He was clearly voicing an opinion that he had voiced many times before.

Mrs Wallace's response seemed equally automatic. 'Nonsense! How could she?'

Mr Wallace inclined towards MacGregor. 'Things got so bad that, in the end, we went to the doctor.'

'For advice,' said Mrs Wallace. 'And to the vicar. Fat lot of good either of them did.'

'Well, we don't go to church, of course,' said Mr Wallace dully.

'We go to the doctor!' snapped his wife. 'And what's the good of telling us seventeen years later that we should have told her she was adopted from the start?'

'They did advise us to be patient with her,' said Mr Wallace, miserably addressing the room at large.

'We *were* patient with her!' stormed Mrs Wallace, the tears gushing forth again. 'And look where it got us! Our Pearl running away from home and getting herself pregnant and dead! If that's what being patient gets you, I'm sorry we bothered!'

MacGregor himself was getting bored with the Wallaces. With some difficulty he managed to extract the only piece of factual information which they seemed capable of supplying: the name and address of the adoption society from which they had got Pearl.

'Of course I bloody well noticed!' roared Dover when, some fifteen minutes later, they were back in the police car and speeding on their way to Frenchy Botham and a promised supper of boiled brisket and dumplings, with bread-and-butter pudding and gorgonzola cheese to follow. 'Wadderyethink I am? A bloody moron or something?'

Luckily MacGregor knew a rhetorical question when he heard one and didn't feel obliged to answer.

'It might,' opined Dover, sinking several of his chins deep into the collar of his overcoat and tipping his bowler hat well down over his eyes, 'be the break-through we've been looking for.'

MacGregor felt he had to play Devil's Advocate. 'Just because the adoption society where Pearl Wallace came from is in Birmingham, sir, it doesn't mean that that's where she was telephoning. She could have been ringing thousands of other places in Birmingham when she made that call from Ermengilda's Kitchen. It's probably just a coincidence, sir.'

'I don't believe in coincidences,' rumbled Dover. 'Besides, it'll be easy enough to check.' He sniggered softly to himself. 'Like father, like son, eh?'

'Sir?'

Dover's face, glowing milkily in the lights of passing cars, emerged momentarily from its cocoon of greasy, dark-blue abercrombie. ''Strewth, I should have thought even you could see that. She was following in her mother's footsteps, wasn't she?'

'Following in her mother's footsteps, sir?' MacGregor had had a long, tiring day, too and he wasn't at his brightest.

'Oh, use your brains, laddie!' snorted Dover impatiently. 'Look, she runs away from home and heads for the bright lights. Before you can say "Women's Lib", she's got herself enrolled in the Pudding Club. Well, if that isn't the spitting image of Mum, I don't know what is.'

'And then she starts thinking about having the child adopted,' said MacGregor slowly, trying the idea on for size. 'Again, as her mother did.'

'If you ask me, she didn't have much blooming choice. I'll lay odds there was no question of marriage and she'd not be likely to get much help from her adoptive mother and father, would she? That leaves abortion or adoption.'

'She could have kept the child, sir.'

'And I,' scoffed Dover with a rare flash of insight, 'could become Chief Bleeding Commissioner of the Metropolitan Police! I'll tell you one thing, though, laddie.'

MacGregor waited with well-controlled eagerness for the next pearl of wisdom.

'It wouldn't surprise me if she didn't tell these people at this Bullfrog place who the father was.'

'It's *Bullrush*, actually, sir.' MacGregor had a tidy mind and just couldn't stop himself. 'The Bullrush Interdenominational Adoption Society.'

'What I said!' grunted Dover. 'You mark my words, if she's told anybody who Young Lochinvar is, she's told them.'

'If she's told anybody, sir,' agreed MacGregor doubtfully. He was not blessed with Dover's bounding optimism. 'Actually, sir, I don't quite see how all this is going to fit in.'

'With what?'

'Well, with what we've been assuming up to now, sir.'

Dover submerged himself even deeper into his overcoat. 'Such as what?' he demanded in a voice that was muffled but menacing.

'Well, sir, if Pearl Wallace was intending to have the baby adopted, what was she doing in Frenchy Botham?'

The response came as surely as night follows day. 'Frenchy Botham?'

'Where her dead body was found, sir.'

'She was gunning for the father. 'Strewth, I thought we'd settled all that bloody years ago. Blackmailing him or whatever.'

'But, if the child was going to be adopted, sir,' ventured MacGregor a little diffidently, 'would she still be going to all that trouble to contact the father?'

'Why the hell not?'

MacGregor didn't quite know. 'It's just that she would seem to be in a stronger position to put pressure on the father, sir, if she was intending to keep the child.'

Dover yawned noisily and thought quickly. 'The father wouldn't know she was going to have it adopted, would he?' he asked triumphantly. 'She could spin him any old yarn. Look, laddie, stop picking at it! We've got the picture clear now and I'm buggered if I'm going to have you keep messing it up. The putative father' – Dover was rather pleased with this piece of jargon so he repeated it – 'the putative father passes through What-do-you-call-it . . .'

'Barford-in-the-Meadow, sir.'

'. . . and has it off with young What's-her-name . . .'

'Pearl Wallace, sir.'

'. . . leaving her holding the baby. Somehow or other she's got hold of his address. Or partial address.' Dover corrected himself quickly as he sensed rather than saw that MacGregor's mouth was opening to remind him about the telephone kiosk on Chapminster railway station. 'She follows him, demands money or marriage or whatever, and he smacks her over the head with whatever blunt instrument he happens to have handy. Got it now? Right, well' – Dover sank once more into his coat collar – 'I'm just going to have a quiet think about – er – things, so belt up for a bit!'

Inspector Walters turned up at The Laughing Dog again just as Dover and MacGregor were finishing their supper. In Dover's case it had been the usual 'feeding-time at the zoo' spectacle, and Inspector Walters didn't appreciate what he'd been spared by arriving only in time for the coffee. Not that the Inspector relished this business of trying to hold conferences across gravy-bespattered tablecloths, but it seemed to be the only time he could ever get hold of these Scotland Yard men. And this conference had to be held because Inspector Walter's Chief Constable was beginning to get quite neurotic about not knowing what the hell was going on.

Dover, mindful of past favours, greeted Inspector Walters warmly. The local chap had proved himself more than willing to stand his round, and Dover didn't ask more than that of anyone. 'What, no brandy tonight, Inspector?' he had called out jovially.

Inspector Walters had been half-hoping that it was somebody else's turn to push the boat out. 'Oh, sorry,' he muttered awkwardly and shuffled off to rectify the omission.

With the Inspector's drinks and the sergeant's cigarettes, Dover was quite content to sit on over the supper table while MacGregor gave a somewhat optimistic account of the progress so far in the case of the murder of Pearl Wallace. Inspector Walters, while not bursting a gut with enthusiasm, had to admit that some progress had indeed been made. The identity of the dead girl had finally been established and that, Inspector Walters grudgingly conceded, was marginally better than the proverbial slap in the belly with a wet fish.

'And now you're off again tomorrow to Birmingham to see the people at the adoption society, are you?' he asked unhappily. The Chief Constable would run amuck when he heard this. 'I suppose that'll take all day, too?'

'It's a long way,' MacGregor pointed out, put on the defensive by Inspector Walter's obvious disapproval.

'Wouldn't a telephone call do just as well? After all, you said yourself, you don't know for sure that Pearl Wallace was ever in touch with them at all. She could have been ringing anybody on that Birmingham number and it may have nothing to do with her death at all.'

'I've got a feeling,' declared Dover, who wasn't going to be deprived of another day joy-riding round the countryside in a nice comfy car. 'In my gut.' He belched comfortably. 'There's a connection there all right.'

Inspector Walters knew a case of malingering when he saw one and remained sceptical. 'I still can't help feeling that the solution to the murder lies here in Frenchy Botham, sir,' he said stubbornly. 'After all, she did come here – half-way across the country, it seems. And she did ask the way to The Grove – and that's where the dead body was found. To my way of thinking it stands out a mile that somebody in The Grove killed her – or at the very least knows a hell of a lot more about her than he's admitting.'

'Me, I've learned to distrust the obvious,' pontificated Dover, trying to convey at the same time the message that it wouldn't take much to put him right off Inspector Blooming Walters. 'Result of a lifetime's experience. And now' – he bestowed an avuncular beam on his two young companions – 'how about the same again, eh?'

MacGregor went off to do the honours this time, and Dover skilfully turned defence into attack though he was not actually feeling entirely himself. He pointed an accusing finger more or less in the direction of Inspector Walters. 'And what 'bout you, matie? What've you been doing with yourself all day, eh? Been handing out bloody parking tickets?'

Inspector Walters repudiated the charge indignantly. 'I'm

not Traffic!' he protested. 'I'm CID like yourself, sir. And I've been busy all day on the enquiries you asked me to make.'

'Is that so?' Dover's eyes crossed most disconcertingly as he raised his empty glass hopefully to his lips.

Inspector Walters dragged a handful of papers out of his pocket and deposited them on the table in front of him. 'You remember, sir? You asked me to check and see if any of the residents in The Grove had got criminal records. Well, I've got the results here.'

'Good for you!' applauded Dover, paying more attention to trying to lick round the inside of his glass. 'Well done!'

'And I think you'll be surprised to learn, sir, that most of 'em have.'

'Not me,' mumbled Dover gloomily. 'I've got past being surprised at anything, I have. Ah!' He turned happily to welcome MacGregor who was back with fresh supplies.

'I'll get rid of those first, sir,' said Inspector Walters, 'who have led blameless lives of undetected crime. Then we can concentrate on the bastards who were stupid enough to get caught. OK, sir?'

'OK!' agreed Dover, absentmindedly commandeering the whole tray of drinks. 'Carry on, laddie! I'm all ears!'

MacGregor resumed his place at the table and got his notebook out. Had he left it too late, he wondered hopelessly, to train as a dentist or an income tax inspector?

13

'Actually,' began Inspector Walters as Dover refreshed himself audibly with a mouthful of Three Star, 'there's only a couple of them who aren't, as we say, known to the police. That's old Miss Charlotte Henty-Harris and young Mrs Bones. They're both clean. Now, we haven't had time to do much about Mademoiselle Blanchette Foucher, the Bones's current au pair girl, but I've been in touch with the French police. Frankly, though, I don't expect anything startling to turn up there, but it never does any harm to be thorough.'

Dover seemed to be experiencing some difficulty in getting both his eyes to function in harmony. He also appeared somewhat confused. 'What the hell's he nattering on about?'

The appeal was addressed to MacGregor who attempted to explain. 'Inspector Walters has been checking to see if any of the suspects has a criminal record, sir.'

'Cheeky bugger!' exploded Dover, his eyes bulging indignantly. 'Why doesn't he mind his own bloody business?'

'You asked him to, sir.'

Dover glared round pugnaciously. 'What about this joker here?'

Inspector Walters's quiet smile of self-satisfaction had faded long ago. 'What joker where, sir?'

'Here!' repeated Dover. 'You gone deaf now or something? The landlord of this pub. Have you checked him?'

Inspector Walters glanced uneasily at MacGregor. Was this some sort of leg-pull. 'Mr Plum, sir? I didn't realize you wanted him checked. Is he a suspect?'

'He's Number One in my book!' said Dover roundly.

'Is he, sir?' Inspector Walters was not acquainted with the Dover Method of Detection and was thus at something of a loss.

'Look, laddie,' said Dover, apparently willing to share his expertise with those less fortunately endowed, 'who was it who turned our attention to The Grove in the first bloody place?'

'The girl's body was found there, too, sir,' said MacGregor, sticking his oar in where it definitely wasn't wanted.

Dover paid scant heed to the interruption. 'It was Plum, wasn't it? He was the one who came rushing forward with this cock-and-bull story about the girl coming in here and asking for The Grove. That's what set all you numskulls combing The Grove for the murderer in the first place, isn't it? Well, just you suppose it's Plum himself who's the father of What's-her-name's unborn child and see where that gets you! It gets you to him killing her and dumping her body in The Grove, to which he then cunningly misdirects our attention.' Dover refreshed himself after his labours with the entire contents of one of the glasses on the tray.

'Good God!' said Inspector Walters faintly. 'But, there's no evidence to connect Mr Plum with the murder, is there, sir?'

'There's no evidence not to connect him with it, either,' pointed out Dover. As an argument it was unanswerable. 'And I'll bet you haven't even checked his alibi.'

'His alibi, sir?'

'For the night the girl was killed, you moron! Believe you me, if Plum can't account for every second of his time, *with witnesses*, he's for the bloody high jump!'

MacGregor felt it was time to take a hand again. 'But, if Mr Plum is lying, sir, we don't actually know when the girl was killed. We've nothing to go on but the medical evidence, and you know how vague that is.' MacGregor was feeling very cross. He knew Dover was only doing it for devilment but, still, Mr Plum's evidence shouldn't have been accepted quite so complacently at its face value. That was the trouble with Dover, thought Mac-Gregor bitterly. Once in a blue moon and by some sheer fluke, the old fool got something right. Of course, the idea that Mr Plum was involved in the murder of Pearl Wallace was quite absurd – the mere fact that it was Dover who'd thought of it proved how absurd it was. Nonetheless it should have been investigated. It would have to be investigated now, just in case. MacGregor found himself back in the middle of his old nightmare where he was being outsmarted by Dover.

He closed his notebook with a snap. 'I'll go and ask a few questions right away, sir,' he said. 'Somebody else in the pub may have seen the girl that night or ...'

' Fetch him in here !' commanded Dover, upon whom alcohol seemed to be having a rejuvenating effect. 'Ring the bell for him !'

MacGregor knew that Dover hated letting him go off on his own and so, all unsuspecting, he rang the bell.

In a few moments Mr Plum duly poked his head round the door.

Dover took immediate charge of the situation. 'My sergeant here wants to ask you a question,' he announced, grinning wickedly all over his fat and sweaty face.

Mr Plum responded with equal good humour. 'Oh, yes, sir,' he said cheerfully, 'and what question might that be?'

' He wants to know if you'll bring us another round of drinks !' howled Dover, all but rupturing himself with his extravagant expressions of puerile mirth. 'Large ones, this time !'

By rights there should at that moment have been another nasty murder in Frenchy Botham, but MacGregor managed to restrain himself. One day, he promised himself, he would really go for Dover with the utmost malice aforethought – but not in front of two witnesses. He waited with seething impatience while a highly amused Mr Plum fetched in yet more booze and while Dover, still laughing helplessly, mopped away at his eyes with his table napkin and finally blew his nose on it. Inspector Walters sat there with his head well tucked in, wondering what the hell to make of it all. He'd come across some damned crack-brained coppers in his time, but this fat old bastard took the bloody biscuit.

Order and decorum were, however, eventually restored and the question as to whether or not Mr Plum was a murderer was allowed to remain in abeyance. Dover lit up one of MacGregor's cigarettes and exhorted a bemused Inspector Walters to stop sitting there like a constipated hen and get on with it.

Inspector Walters pulled himself together. 'Oh, yes, the criminal records, sir!' He scrabbled through his papers. 'Well, as I was saying, Miss Henty-Harris has no previous form, which is not surprising, really, as old Sir Perceval would have turned her out of the house if she'd even thought about wandering off the straight and narrow. He was a right narrow-minded old devil, he was. God rest him, of course. Now, who's next? Ah, yes, young Mr and Mrs Bones ...'

'Bloody little bastard!' snarled Dover, proving that there were some things at least that he neither forgot nor forgave.

'Mrs Bones, sir, has never been in any trouble with the Law but her husband, Peter Bones, has had three convictions for speeding. None of 'em very serious and spread out, admittedly, over the last ten years, but infringements of the Law nonetheless.'

A lump of ash dropped off Dover's cigarette and made its small contribution to the debris which graced the front of his waistcoat.

Inspector Walters went soldiering on. 'Brigadier Gough. He's the man, sir, who lives in the house next door to the one the girl's body was found at. His wife is the religious lady, the one who wants to become a parson and ...'

'I know!' snarled Dover, who didn't care for being patronized. 'Get on with it, for God's sake!'

'Well, Brigadier Gough is actually quite interesting, sir. He was fined pretty heavily a couple of years ago for failing to stop after being involved in a road traffic accident. He was in collision with a laundry van near a bus stop just outside Chapminster.'

'And?'

'Well, he hadn't a snowball's chance of getting away with it, sir. There were half a dozen eye-witnesses, three of whom took his number. When the case came to court he pleaded guilty and offered no excuses or explanations.'

Dover shifted impatiently in his chair. 'Why don't you get to the bloody point?'

'Brigadier Gough's a real stickler for law and order, sir. I believe there was once some question of him becoming a J P himself. In any case, he certainly isn't a hit-and-run driver.'

'So?'

'He'd got somebody else in the car with him, sir. A young female, I understand. This information, being irrelevant, didn't come out in open court, nor did the fact that his wife was away from home at the time. Demonstrating outside Lambeth Palace or chaining herself to the altar rails in York Minster or something.

Dover grasped the implications with gratifying speed. 'I said right from the start that man was a womanizer! Lecherous old devil! Chasing around after kids young enough to be his daughters! Well, he's gone a sight too far this time!'

'I suppose,' said MacGregor, who could also see the possibilities, 'that Mrs Gough is away from home quite often?'

'Quite frequently, I understand,' agreed Inspector Walters. 'So, what with one thing and another, it's not surprising that the Brigadier's eyes wander occasionally. I mean, who'd want to be married to the sort of woman that wants to be a bishop? Mind you,' he added, selecting another of his sheets of paper, 'Mrs Esmond Gough's a pretty lively specimen, all things considered. She's got more blooming form than a Derby winner!' He looked across at Dover. 'You don't want me to read it all out, do you, sir?'

Dover had no doubts. 'Not bloody likely!'

'Actually it's just a series of charges of breaches of the peace, causing an obstruction, insulting behaviour, one assaulting the police and resisting arrest, and one charge of indecent behaviour in St Jude's Church, Hornfield Green, under the Ecclesiastical Court Jurisdiction Act, 1880.' Inspector Walters rattled his list off. 'You may remember that last one, sir? A couple of years ago. It created quite a stir at the time. Seems the vicar at this St Jude's Church didn't go much on the idea of lady parsons and was saying so from the pulpit when Mrs Esmond Gough and two or three of her supporters attacked him physically with their handbags. It was later claimed in their defence when the case came to trial that the subsequent debagging of the vicar on the sanctuary steps was entirely accidental.'

'Has she ever been sent to prison?' asked MacGregor, succumbing to pure vulgar curiosity.

Inspector Walters shook his head. 'No. She's never even been given a suspended sentence, if it comes to that. Just bound over and fines. I think the thing is they don't want to make a martyr out of her. She's a big enough damned nuisance without that.'

'Silly cow!' grunted Dover. 'That the lot?'

'Oh, no, sir! We've got several more suspects to deal with.'

'In that case,' said Dover, who prided himself on never missing a trick, 'I think we'd better have another little drink. It's thirsty work, talking.' He pushed his glass impartially between his two juniors, indicating that he didn't give a monkey's which one of them bought the next round.

When things had settled down again and Dover had raised a purely conventional objection about the embarrassment of drinking alone, Inspector Walters moved on to the Talbots and MacGregor reminded Dover that Mr Talbot was the bank manager.

'He goes in for seances, you know,' said Inspector Walters disparagingly. 'Table tapping and spirit voices. Ectoplasm, too, I shouldn't wonder. It's an open secret round here. We've known about the crazy goings-on for donkey's years.'

'Actually, we had discovered that for ourselves,' said MacGregor loftily. 'In fact, we've even considered the possibility that these arcane meetings might have provided a motive for Pearl Wallace's murder.'

Inspector Walter's eyebrows rose. 'What? A sort of human sacrifice? Blimey, I thought you needed a virgin for that.'

'That wasn't quite what we had in mind,' said MacGregor. 'We simply thought that the girl might have inadvertently stumbled onto the orgy or whatever was going on. Then Talbot or somebody killed her so as to prevent their secret getting out.'

'That sounds a bit far-fetched, sergeant.'

MacGregor's face showed that he hadn't wasted all his time in Dover's company. ' I know it does !' he snapped. ' But Talbot is a bank manager. Maybe he didn't think it would do his career much good if people thought his financial decisions were being guided by spirit voices. Anyhow ' – he got his irritation under control – ' you were telling us about Mr Talbot's criminal record. I presume it doesn't amount to much ?'

' Illegal parking,' said Inspector Walters sulkily.

' I see.'

' In Soho,' said Inspector Walters more cheerfully. ' When he was supposed to be attending a weekend conference on banking in Doncaster.'

' Interesting,' admitted MacGregor.

' It shows that he's another one who might be keen on les girls, in a mild sort of way.'

MacGregor sighed. ' The trouble is, sir, that we've got almost too many people who might have been mixed up with Pearl Wallace and had a reason for killing her. The case is littered with motives. Or possible motives. What we're short of is hard evidence. So far we've not turned up one single fact to connect Pearl Wallace with this part of the world in general, never mind this village in particular. And as for trying to pin the job on anybody living in The Grove ... well !' MacGregor shrugged his shoulders despairingly before knuckling down to the job once more. ' That's Mr Talbot for illegal parking, then. Now, is anything known about his wife ?'

' She's been done for shop-lifting.'

' Where ?'

' In Chapminster. Her solicitor presented a classic case and she virtually got away with it. You know – middle-aged woman, a cry for help, veiled hints about a lack of understanding on the part of her husband. In the end she got a conditional discharge on the understanding that she went to a Marriage Guidance Counsellor. That might,' said Inspector Walters moodily, ' tie in with old Talbot seeking solace in Soho.'

' It might,' said MacGregor without much interest. He was beginning to think longingly of his bed. ' Is that the lot ?'

'There's Clifford de la Poche.' Inspector Walters stifled a yawn on his own behalf. 'We nabbed him once for forgetting to renew his dog licence. Otherwise the beggar's been too clever for us. Still, we'll get him one day. One of those dratted choirboys is sure to shop him sooner or later, however well he bribes 'em.'

'I don't remember a dog,' said MacGregor wearily.

'He got rid of it. It was a Jack Russell bitch. Which brings us,' said Inspector Walters with an apologetic grin, 'to the last one on my list: Mrs Yarrow.'

'The charwoman?'

'You'd better not let her hear you calling her that!'

'What's she been up to?'

'She just happens to be the only person connected with this business – if you can call it a connection because she'd been home for a couple of hours before Pearl Wallace appeared on the scene – she's the only one with any violence in her background. She attacked the lady of the house where she was working over at Horwill. Went for her with a poker. The lady had criticized the way Mrs Yarrow cleaned brass.'

MacGregor raised a very faint grin. 'What did they charge her with? Justifiable attempted murder?'

'Not quite! She got a good ticking off from the Bench and was bound over to keep the peace. It was her first offence. And her last, if it comes to that.'

'And that's the lot?'

Inspector Walters agreed that it was. 'Not much help, I'm afraid.'

It was true but MacGregor, given half a chance, was quite a kindly lad. 'Oh, well, every little helps, sir, and you never know – we might have found that one of the suspects had already committed murder. You know what it's like these days. Some killers are out and back in society in a matter of weeks.'

Inspector Walters nodded. 'Bloody disgusting, I call it,' he agreed as he began to gather himself together for his departure. 'Well, I'd better be pushing off home before the old woman starts thinking she's a widow. Where is it you're off to tomorrow? Birmingham?' He shook his head. 'I still think the answer's to be found here in Frenchy Botham.' He looked at Dover for a brief moment. Of course, the chap could just be resting his eyes against the light but ... 'Oh, by the way, I almost forgot. The Chief Constable would like a word sometime. Just to say "hello", you know, and find out how you're getting on. At your convenience, naturally, but he'd like it to be tomorrow morning. Maybe you could call in before you leave?'

Dover couldn't have picked a better moment to fall off his chair. It saved MacGregor the trouble of finding an evasive answer to an inconvenient question, and it happened before Inspector Walters had left. This enabled MacGregor to get some assistance in lugging the paralytic, seventeen-and-a-quarter stone Detective Chief Inspector upstairs to bed. The incident proved something of an education for Inspector Walters. Until he'd helped disrobe Dover and seen his underwear, the local man hadn't realized what a sheltered life he'd lived.

'Just time for a night-cap!' whispered MacGregor as they thankfully closed the door on Dover's stentorian snores.

Inspector Walters, having just had a brutal lesson on the dangers of strong drink, was dubious.

'Come on!' urged MacGregor. 'We've earned it. Besides, I want to make a few enquiries about Mr Plum, our helpful host.' He led the way downstairs. 'I hate to admit it, but old Dover was quite right. We have only got Plum's unsupported word for it that Pearl Wallace ever mentioned The Grove at all.'

14

The Last Trump apart, there was probably only one thing that would have induced Dover to rise from his bed of pain the following morning, and by some miracle MacGregor came armed with it.

'The Chieth Conthtable?' repeated Dover, taking out his top set and blearily examining it for unfair wear and tear. 'You can thuff that for a lark, laddie!' He munched his teeth defiantly back into place.

'Half past nine in his office, sir,' said MacGregor, really putting the frighteners on. 'And he wants a full progress report.'

''Strewth!' moaned Dover, rolling miserably over and hiding his head in the blankets. 'Tell him I'm not well. Unfit for duty. Gastric flu. The runs. Typhoid.'

MacGregor grinned to himself. 'He'd be round like a shot, sir,' he pointed out. 'With a police surgeon.'

Dover unveiled a face pallid with fear, constipation and hangover. 'Save me!' he begged.

'I think even the Chief Constable would be prepared to admit that our trip to Birmingham should take priority, sir,' lied MacGregor smoothly. 'We can't be expected to postpone serious investigations for something that doesn't amount to much more than a courtesy call. If we were to make an early start ...' He saw that Dover was hoisting the white flag. Birmingham it was! 'Shall I ask them to serve you breakfast up here, sir?'

Dover shook his head and wished he hadn't. 'No breakfast, laddie!' he gasped – and showed how the mighty were fallen.

They eventually reached Birmingham after lengthy halts at every public convenience en route. In spite of this, Dover's first question when he arrived at the premises of the Bullrush Interdenominational Adoption Society was where was the lavatory?

Luckily Mrs Vincent had been a social worker for more than thirty years and it took more than the vagaries of Dover's bladder to disconcert her. Indeed, she got Dover's number with commendable speed.

'I suppose I'd better order a large pot of black coffee,' she remarked acidly as she and MacGregor watched Dover disappearing at an anxious trot down the long and highly polished corridor.

But Dover was gradually regaining his health and strength and by the time he returned to Mrs Vincent's office he'd at least found his appetite again. While MacGregor plodded conscientiously through the preliminaries, Dover equally conscientiously gobbled down every biscuit on the coffee tray. It was only when he'd finished these and eaten all the lump sugar as well that he paid much attention to the rest of the proceedings.

Mrs Vincent was handing the photograph of the dead girl back to MacGregor. 'Yes, that's her all right. Pearl Wallace. Poor child!'

MacGregor tucked the photograph away. 'And she came here to see you on Saturday, the eighth of this month?'

'That's right, sergeant. She'd telephoned earlier. I wouldn't normally have given her an interview on a Saturday but I wasn't free earlier and she seemed so distressed that I felt I had to make an exception. After all, it isn't the first time and this isn't a five-day-a-week job.'

'She came to see you about having her baby adopted?'

Mrs Vincent stared unhappily at MacGregor for quite a long time. 'I'm so sorry, sergeant,' she said with a rueful laugh. 'It's just that I'm so used to total confidentiality in my work that I'm finding it rather difficult to break old habits.'

'This is a murder case, madam,' MacGregor reminded her. 'Anything not strictly relevant to our enquiries will, however, be treated with as much discretion as ...'

'Oh, yes, I'm only hesitating, sergeant, not refusing. I've taken the trouble to clarify my position with our Head Office and they have authorized me to give you full co-operation. That still doesn't mean I enjoy doing it, of course.'

MacGregor thought Mrs Vincent was really rather nice and he rewarded her by giving her one of his special twinkles. 'It may help us find the girl's murderer.'

Mrs Vincent sighed. 'I suppose so. Now, you want to know why she came to see me. It wasn't anything to do with having any baby of hers adopted, I'm afraid. She simply wanted as much information as we could give her about her own natural mother. Pearl Wallace, as you probably know, was offered for adoption through us some eighteen years ago. I wasn't here at the time, as it happens, but we have records. We are obliged by law to keep them for at least twenty-five years, so the papers relating to Miss Wallace were readily available.'

'Here, just a minute!' Dover broke in pugnaciously. 'I thought everything to do with adoptions was top secret.'

'It's this new law that's been passed, sir,' explained MacGregor. He prided himself on keeping abreast of current affairs and read the *Daily Telegraph* nearly every day. He could, therefore, be forgiven if he tended to expound at length to such as Dover who rarely got beyond the headlines in the *Sun* and always went to the toilet when the television news came on. 'From now on, adopted children can, when they reach the age of eighteen, obtain details of their birth, if they want to. And I believe ' – he glanced for confirmation to Mrs Vincent – 'that the legislation is retrospective.' Dover wasn't very good at thirteen letter words so MacGregor explained further. 'That means, sir, that it's not only children adopted *after* the passing of this new Act who can apply to see their birth certificates and so on. Those adopted *before* it was passed have been given the same rights.'

'And that's where our troubles begin,' said Mrs Vincent.

Dover was still truculent. 'I'm blowed if I see why!'

'Well, take this poor girl, Pearl Wallace.' Mrs Vincent had found from long experience that people with low IQs did better with concrete examples. 'When she was adopted eighteen years ago, everything was done in an atmosphere of the greatest secrecy. The natural mother gave up all her rights. She usually never met the adopting parents or knew their name or where they lived. The adopting parents, too, were given only the most generalized and meagre details about the child's background. A real effort was made, you see, to wipe out the past and to get the baby's new identity established as quickly and securely as possible. All this was done primarily for the sake of the child, but it also allowed the natural mother to make a complete break with *her* past. She was free to make a fresh start, if that's what she wanted.'

'So why've they changed things?' demanded Dover, scowling horribly.

'Some adopted children want to know who their real parents were,' said Mrs Vincent simply. 'Not all of them, but some. Occasionally the desire becomes obsessive. This new law was designed to help them. However, in recognizing the undoubted rights of the adopted child to information about himself, the rights of the natural mother to anonymity have been sacrificed. Girls who offer their babies for adoption today know what they're in for. Pearl Wallace's mother eighteen years ago was, on the other hand, given every assurance by the courts, by society and by us that she would never see or hear of her child again.'

Dover grasped the implications. 'Some women,' he sniggered, 'are in for a nasty shock when their little bastards come waltzing up the garden path shouting, "Mummie!" Well' – he sat back and folded his arms in instant judgement – 'serves 'em bloody well right! They should have behaved themselves in the first place.'

Mrs Vincent very sensibly decided not to get involved in a slanging match with Dover. Their views on unmarried mothers were poles apart, and no expenditure of logic or emotion was likely to bring them any closer. She turned back to MacGregor who did, of course, tend to look better and better the more one saw of Dover. 'From our point of view, then, Pearl Wallace was just one of many. We've dealt with dozens of these cases. Children who were adopted through this Society and who apply to us for any information we may have about their real parentage.'

'Information,' queried MacGregor, who was anxious to get the situation absolutely clear in his own mind, 'which you are required by law to give?'

'Not exactly,' said Mrs Vincent. 'Roughly, what happens is this. The adopted child now has the right to see his original birth certificate but, before even this is allowed, he has to have an interview with a social worker first. This is necessary because some of these adopted children are going through a real crisis of identity. They think that finding their real mother will solve all their problems and usher in the Golden Age. The social worker's job is to point out that such an encounter will produce problems of its own and there is, of course, always the danger that there will be a second rejection by the natural mother which could be even more hurtful than the first. Now, this whole process may take as long as a couple of months and may not, as far as hard facts are concerned, be all that helpful. Any information will be at least eighteen years old and trying to trace the mother from that ... Well, it's usually at this stage that they come to us.'

MacGregor nodded. 'But you are not legally required to help?'

'No, but in practice we do. Some of us are not altogether happy about the situation but I feel that, in today's climate of opinion, we must help if we can. After all, if there is any guilty party in an adoption – which I would dispute – it is certainly not the child.'

Dover was getting restless. MacGregor quickly gave him a cigarette but even this wasn't enough to stop his loud mouth. 'I thought,' he said in an aside which was probably heard quite clearly in Wolverhampton, 'we'd come to find something out about this dead girl, not listen to a blooming lecture. Can't you get her to belt up? She's making my bloody head ache!'

MacGregor twinkled quite hard at Mrs Vincent after this but, somehow, the magic seemed to have gone. This time Mrs Vincent definitely did not twinkle back.

She sat very stiff and upright behind her desk and made her next statement with a certain amount of curtness. 'Pearl Wallace came here for information about her natural mother. I gave her what we had.'

MacGregor wiggled his pencil by way of an interrogative.

'Her mother was a young, unmarried woman of twenty-six,' stated Mrs Vincent, still cold and unbending. 'She either didn't know or wouldn't say who the father was. It appears she wasn't a local girl. She was staying with an aunt and appeared to have come to this part of the world, where she wasn't known, to have the baby.'

MacGregor, realizing that he wasn't going to get the aunt's address without actually asking for it, meekly asked.

Mrs Vincent stared right past him. 'Do you have to have it?'

'I'm afraid so.' MacGregor wrote the address down carefully at Mrs Vincent's dictation. 'And the aunt's name?'

'Kincardine. Mrs Kincardine.'

Dover broke into the exchanges. 'We'll need the name of the blooming mother, too,' he pointed out.

'Jones,' said Mrs Vincent, her lips puckering disdainfully. 'Muriel Jones.'

'*Jones?*' Dover was not one for mincing matters. 'Now pull the other one!' he invited with heavy humour.

Mrs Vincent shuddered. 'That was the name she gave.'

'And you lot accepted it?' asked Dover incredulously.

'Why not? It's a perfectly reasonable name. Why should you assume that it's not genuine?'

Dover sniffed to indicate that he wasn't there to answer questions, thank you very much! 'And what was the girl going to do with all this information of yours? Try and follow it up?'

'One would imagine so.' Mrs Vincent's helpful nature got the better of her and she became fractionally more co-operative. 'She was extremely keen to find her mother, but I was puzzled by her attitude.'

'In what way, madam?' MacGregor got in quickly before Dover could start putting everybody's back up again.

Mrs Vincent sighed, hesitated and frowned. 'I must have dealt with scores of adopted children in my time – teenagers, mostly – who were trying to trace their real parents. They were searching for love, of course. Pearl Wallace wasn't like that.'

'Well, what was she like?' demanded Dover impatiently.

'It struck me that she wasn't trying to find her real mother out of love, but out of hate. I felt she was seeking a confrontation, a show-down. God forgive me, but the idea of blackmail even crossed my mind.'

'Blackmail?' MacGregor looked up. 'Really?'

Dover concentrated on the basics. 'And you didn't know she was pregnant herself?'

Mrs Vincent shook her head. 'No, but it would explain a lot. Pearl implied that she needed help – financial help. Presumably her adopted parents wouldn't or couldn't give it her, and no doubt the father of her child was equally unwilling. That only leaves the real mother, doesn't it?'

'Or the State,' said Dover sourly. 'She could always have got a hand-out there.'

'I think she preferred to try and get it out of her mother,' said Mrs Vincent with some reluctance. 'It would give her more satisfaction.'

'Suppose the real mother refused to pay up? You know – publish and be damned?'

Mrs Vincent looked steadily at MacGregor. 'There'd be trouble,' she said quietly. 'I only saw Pearl Wallace for about three-quarters of an hour but I don't have any doubts about that. She seemed to be nursing a grudge against the whole, wide world.'

Dover and MacGregor took their leave. Back in the cosiness of the police car, Dover took a quick snooze while MacGregor and the driver searched out the village which Pearl Wallace's mother had given as her address.

'There it is, sarge!' The driver jabbed his finger into the dog-eared map. 'Norrisbridge! It's not all that far off. We could be there in ten minutes.' He jerked his head in the direction of the back seat. 'Why don't we just go, eh? If I take it nice and easy we could be there before His Nibs knows what's hit him.'

MacGregor was second to none in his low opinion of Detective Chief Inspector Wilfred Dover, but that didn't mean he was prepared to tolerate disparaging remarks from a lowly police driver. 'Watch it!' he warned and, thanks to Dover, made another enemy for life.

'Pearl Who?' asked Dover, staring dopily at his sergeant.

'The girl whose dead body was found in amongst the bushes at Frenchy Botham, sir!' MacGregor regretted he'd been unable to take the driver's advice and only wake the old fool when they got there.

'Oh, yes.' Dover hoisted himself more or less into the horizontal and gazed vacantly around. 'What are we stopping here for?'

'We were just checking the route to Norrisbridge, sir.' MacGregor snapped his fingers. 'Carry on, driver!'

Dover sullenly watched the suburban landscape flow steadily past the car windows. 'Norrisbridge?'

'Where the dead girl's mother's aunt lived, sir.'

Dover grunted. 'I reckon we're wasting our time over this long-lost mother business,' he grumbled, all but unhinging his jaws in a mighty yawn. 'We've got the broad outlines of the case. Why' – he paused to give the waiting world another look at his tonsils – 'complicate things? I mean,' – he scratched his stomach with a good deal more energy than he ever devoted to detecting – 'that Waifs and Strays woman clinched it as far as I'm concerned.'

'Mrs Vincent, sir?' MacGregor couldn't for the life of him think what Mrs Vincent had said that would confirm Dover's theory that Pearl Wallace had been murdered by the father of her unborn child.

'She said Thingummy-jig was capable of blackmail. Right? Well, all she got wrong was who the victim was. The one that girl tried to put the squeeze on was lover-boy.' He stopped straining his eyes by gawping out of the window and sank back into the cushions. 'You mark my words, laddie! Pound to a penny I'm right!'

15

'I should have gone again,' admitted Dover in a rare orgy of self-criticism, 'back at that bloody orphanage place. Well, don't just stand there like a lemon!' he urged. 'Ring again! Use your bloody boot if they won't answer!'

'They seem to be out, sir,' said MacGregor, disloyally reflecting that it had been many a long year since Dover had been so keen to get an interview.

'Nonsense!' snarled Dover, looking more worried than angry.

'It looks all shut up to me, sir.' This contribution came from the police driver who had emerged from the car to stretch his legs.

They were all standing in front of a row of mean little semi-detached houses, most of which had been further disfigured by the addition of such improvements as heliotrope front doors, picture windows and wrought-iron door furniture made of plastic. Number Twenty-seven, the house they were interested in, was however still untouched and in the ignoble state its jobbing builder had intended.

The police driver – the only one of the trio who had retained the common touch – collared a passing neighbour. 'Anybody at home at Number Twenty-seven, love?'

The neighbour took in the situation at a glance, though she

was slightly puzzled by the fat man in the bowler hat who kept hopping about from one foot to the other. 'Come to take him away, have you?' she asked confidently. 'Well, not before time, if you ask me. You'll have to break in, you know. He's not opened that door for the last five years to my certain knowledge. Except to Mrs O'Brien and it's no good you trying to get hold of her because she's gone off to Morecambe for the day to see her sister.' The neighbour neatly eluded the police driver's restraining grasp and went rejoicing on her way.

Dover, whose predicament was growing acute, turned on the police driver. 'You bloody moron!' he howled. 'Why didn't you ask her if I could use her place?'

The police driver was unversed in the eccentricities of Dover's physiology and didn't know quite what to make of this outburst. Before he could ask for enlightenment, though, MacGregor broke in with some good news.

'It's all right, I think somebody's coming!'

It was only the letter-box that opened.

'Bugger off!' advised a wavering voice which had long since decided that the best way of dealing with visiting humanity was via a two-inch thick door. 'Bugger off or I'll set the Alsatian on you!'

MacGregor bent double and tried to project all his persuasive charm through that narrow slit. 'Er – could we just have a word, sir?'

'Bugger off!' came the amiable response. 'I've already sent for the bobbies!'

MacGregor produced his warrant card and held it out to the letter-box. 'We *are* the police, sir!'

The yellowed eye, which was all that was visible of a very misanthropic old man, blinked contemptuously. 'Any idiot can get hold of a bit of cardboard! Go on, push off! I've got a loaded shot-gun here,' he added with peculiar malice.

'Break the bloody door down!' ordered Dover, taking up a position well clear of any possible line of fire. 'Don't waste your time talking to him!'

But MacGregor bent down to the letter-box again. This time

his honeyed words were greeted by a series of blasts on a police whistle, interspersed with unlikely appeals to even more unlikely accomplices.

'You ready with your pitchfork, Tom?' screamed the unseen occupant of Number Twenty-seven. 'Got the machine-gun loaded, Bert? Stack the hand-grenades by the bedroom window, Harry, and tell Jack to keep his rifle trained on this young devil by the door!'

MacGregor's head was spinning with the noise, to which had been added some frantic banging on a dustbin lid, and he turned round to tell Dover that in his opinion the situation was hopeless. But Dover wasn't there. Before MacGregor could make further enquiries about the current whereabouts of his lord and master, however, that familiar and gruesome figure came waddling back round the side of the house.

''Strewth, that's better!' puffed Dover. He now seemed prepared to take a rosier view of life.

All MacGregor could do was pray, for the umpteenth time, that the earth beneath his feet would open up and swallow him. He gestured helplessly towards the back of the house. 'Oh, sir, you haven't?'

'Garn!' blustered Dover. 'Don't be such a bloody little namby-pamby! Besides, I read somewhere it is supposed to be good for cabbages. Now, how far have we got here? 'Strewth' – he paused to listen to the shrill battle cries and Red Indian war whoops which were proceeding unabated from behind the still-closed door of Number Twenty-seven – 'he'll be doing himself a mischief if he keeps on like that!'

'And we'll be accused of police brutality,' agreed MacGregor bitterly.

Dover was always ready to cut his losses. 'He probably doesn't know anything anyhow. Let's leave him to it.'

MacGregor didn't like admitting he was beaten but, on this occasion, he was inclined to agree with Dover. 'I don't suppose Pearl Wallace would have got any information out of him, either, sir,' he observed as he trailed behind his lord and master back to the car. 'I think we can assume that Mrs Kincardine is no longer living at this address and, if the old boy in there does know where she is, he's not telling.'

Dover began to squeeze himself into the back seat of the car. 'Told you it was a waste of time.'

'Maybe if I just asked around, sir?'

Dover was concentrating on making himself comfortable. 'Nobody'll know anything. It was all nearly twenty years ago.'

'Was you inquiring about Mrs Kincardine?'

The female neighbour, who had previously been accosted by the police driver, had returned from the corner shop with her loaf of sliced bread and had been standing, unnoticed by our eagle-eyed detectives, listening to the greater part of their conversation.

MacGregor turned to her eagerly. 'Yes, we were, as a matter of fact. Did you know her?'

'Oh, yes.' The female neighbour rested her shopping basket companionably on the bonnet of the police car. 'We've lived at Number Eighteen for nigh on thirty-two years. I knew Mrs Kincardine quite well. Like I told that girl, we were never what you might call close friends, but we never missed speaking. She moved ten years ago. No—I tell a lie—it must have been eleven.'

MacGregor chivalrously restrained himself from grabbing the good woman and shaking the information out of her. 'What girl?'

'I don't know what girl, do I? She never told me her name and I didn't ask. Well, you don't, do you?'

MacGregor whipped out his picture of Pearl Wallace and handed it across with absurdly trembling fingers. Were they really going to be lucky at last? 'Is this the girl you're talking about?'

The female neighbour – her name was Mrs Shackleton – agreed that it was. 'But she didn't look like that. Here' – Mrs Shackleton pushed the photograph back into MacGregor's hands with a shudder of distaste – 'she's not dead, is she?'

'I'm afraid she is.'

'Well, I'll go to our house!' Mrs Shackleton swayed a little on her feet. 'I think I'd like to sit down,' she said unsteadily. 'I've come over all faint.'

They put her in the back seat next to Dover who was persuaded with considerable difficulty to reduce his occupancy of the available space to a mere two-thirds.

Mrs Shackleton, it transpired, was in the habit of carrying a small flask of British Ruby Sherry for just such emergencies. When she had 'wet her lips', as she put it, and, much to Dover's fury, tucked the flask away in her handbag, she pronounced herself fit and willing to continue with her story.

'She was just like you lot,' she began. 'Hammering away on that silly old devil's door and getting nothing but whistles and howls and bangings for her pains. His brain's gone, you know. Senile decay, my husband says it is. They ought to put him away, really. The Welfare keep calling but they never seem to do anything much. Of course, like I said to Mrs O'Brien, as long as she keeps going round and doing for him, they never will. Shame, really, because there's many a young married couple that I know of who'd give their right arms for that house. It wants a bit of doing up, of course, but ....'

'This girl,' said MacGregor. He was forced to stand outside the car and lean in awkwardly through the window.

'She was calling at all the houses in the street but, like I told her, I'm probably the only one who'd remember her at all. These houses have nearly all changed. Well, Mrs Kay at Number Twenty-five might have remembered, but she's away in Benidorm for the week. Lucky for you, eh?' Mrs Shackleton gave Dover a friendly dig in the ribs. 'She lives next door and if she'd seen you relieving yourself in that back garden from her bathroom window she'd have had your guts for garters. Very particular is Mrs Kay.'

'Mrs Kincardine,' prompted MacGregor. 'What did you tell the girl about her?'

'Here, was that girl murdered?' Mrs Shackleton was already fumbling for the sherry in anticipation of the shock. 'What happened?'

'She was struck over the head,' said MacGregor, wondering as the flask rose once again to Mrs Shackleton's pallid lips if she was going to remain sober enough to answer his questions.

'Was she .. ?'

'No,' said MacGregor, relieved at being able to convey some good news.

But any pretext would do for Mrs Shackleton. 'Thank God for that!' she gasped and took another swig. Dover was nearly in tears. 'Now, what was we talking about? Oh, yes, Mrs Kincardine! Well, like I said, I remember her all right. A nice woman, on the whole. We did have that bit of an up-and-a-downer one time about her ginger tom and our budgie but ...'

MacGregor was now past caring what he did to Mrs Shackleton's nerves. He flourished the picture of Pearl Wallace under her nose. 'What did this girl want to know about Mrs Kincardine?'

'Well, nothing, really,' replied Mrs Shackleton, wondering what this good-looking young fellow was getting so aeriated about. 'It was this niece she was really asking about. She had dates and everything but I was blowed if I could think which one she meant. It's all so long ago, isn't it? Mrs Kincardine often had people staying with her. Relations and things. When they'd been ill or bereaved or something like that. I fancy it was in the way of being a little bit of a business for her because her husband can't have left all that much. Mind you, I wouldn't have let such an idea so much as pass my lips at the time.' She turned trustingly to Dover and patted him on the arm. 'It's the Rates, you see, dear. They put 'em up something cruel round here if they even suspect you're using your home for business premises.'

MacGregor's knuckles on the edge of the car window were beginning to turn white and Dover would have blown his top ages ago if he hadn't been hopeful that the British Ruby Sherry would, eventually, be passed round. MacGregor got his cigarettes out in the hope of keeping Dover quiet a bit longer and found that Mrs Shackleton, while not exactly being what you might call a smoker, didn't mind accepting one just to oblige.

As the occupants of the back seat of the car disappeared in a cloud of tobacco smoke, MacGregor resumed his efforts.

'Well, of course she told me she was trying to trace her mother!' said Mrs Shackleton indignantly. 'I don't go around handing out confidential information about my neighbours to every Tom, Dick and Harry that asks, thank you very much!'

'And you couldn't help her?' asked MacGregor, desperate to get at least one solid fact established.

Mrs Shackleton was sufficiently nettled by his tone to give a straight answer. 'No.'

MacGregor was thankfully on the point of declaring the interview closed when the amazing Mrs Shackleton forestalled him yet again.

'Not about her mother, that is. Actually, I do sort of remember her vaguely, with her being in the family way and everything, but I never spoke to her. She kept herself very much to herself. Wore a wedding ring, of course, but you could buy them for next to nothing in Woolworth's in those days. Mrs Kincardine wasn't very forthcoming, either. Of course, you've got to remember they didn't have all these pills and things then.'

MacGregor no long wondered that Dover was frequently tempted to use his fists on witnesses. 'What exactly did you tell Pearl Wallace?'

'About her mother?'

'About *anything*?' wailed MacGregor.

'Well, I told her where to find Mrs Kincardine.'

At that MacGregor finally stopped standing on ceremony with an alacrity that would have warmed Dover's heart, had he been awake to see it. Mrs Shackleton was induced to shell out what she had told Pearl Wallace and was then bundled unceremoniously out of the police car and into oblivion. She didn't have time even to get her flask out before the departing police car enveloped her in a cloud of exhaust fumes.

'The Isle of bloody Man?' yelped Dover, floundering around like a stranded whale as the police driver got rid of his inhibitions and kept his foot well down. 'You must be joking! And you, you bloody maniac' – he leaned forward to deliver a resounding smack on the back of the police driver's head – 'slow down! You'll have us all in the bloody ditch!'

The police driver eased up on the accelerator. 'I thought you were in a hurry, sir,' he muttered sullenly.

'Not to get to the bloody Isle of Man, I'm not!' retorted

Dover, indulging his rapier wit yet again. 'So, if you're thinking of driving us there, forget it!'

Even though he knew that arguing with Dover usually made him still more pig-headed, MacGregor felt he had to try. Murder Squad detectives aren't encouraged to get personally involved in their cases but, whatever the rules, MacGregor felt strangely sorry for Pearl Wallace. In her short life, she had been neither beautiful nor happy nor even lucky. She'd never had much of a break. The least one could do for her now, thought MacGregor, was to put her murderer behind bars. And nothing, MacGregor promised himself, not even the massive inertia of Detective Chief Inspector Wilfred Dover was going to stop him.

'I'm afraid I don't see any alternative, sir.'

Dover scowled. 'Well, I bloody well do, laddie!'

MacGregor gritted his teeth. 'We must follow this through, sir.'

Dover could be equally mulish. 'There's not an atom of proof that the girl's murder had anything to do with her being illegitimate.'

'Sir, we can't ignore the fact that, immediately before her death, Pearl Wallace was trying to trace her real mother. We must follow in her footsteps. If she leads us to a dead end and she didn't find her mother – all right! Then we'll have to start looking elsewhere. But until then ...'

The real trouble was that Dover – to paraphrase the words of that fine old song – was tired of living but scared of flying. He didn't like boats, either. All of which made the prospect of a trip to the Isle of Man look most unattractive.

Naturally Dover marshalled his objections under a horse of a very different colour. 'We can't go haring off to the other end of the world on a wild-goose chase, just like that,' he muttered. 'Think of the expense. We've got the tax-payer's money to think of. These are hard times.'

MacGregor didn't believe a word of it. 'Pearl Wallace,' he said patiently, 'came to Norrisbridge searching for her natural mother. The person she thought could help her was her mother's aunt, Mrs Kincardine. Mrs Kincardine no longer lives in Norrisbridge, but a neighbour, Mrs Shackleton, tells the girl that she left some ten or eleven years ago to live with her son in the Isle of Man. Mrs Shackleton can't remember the address after all these years, of course, but she's pretty sure it wasn't Douglas. She thinks it might be Ramsey. Now, with clues like that Pearl Wallace had every chance of tracking Mrs Kincardine down. The Isle of Man is a comparatively small place and Kincardine's by no means a common name. All I'm saying, sir, is that we must do the same.'

'We can get the Isle of Man police to do it, can't we?' whined Dover.

'Naturally we'll call on them for help in tracing Mrs Kincardine, sir, but I really do feel we ought to conduct the interview with her ourselves.' Grimly MacGregor sought for something that would spur Dover on to greater heights. 'What about Pomeroy Chemicals, sir?'

But Pomeroy Chemicals was now so far back in Dover's past that he'd almost forgotten who they were. The incident of the grossly misused application form seemed to have wiped them completely from his mind.

'Or,' MacGregor went on, seeing that Pomeroy Chemicals had failed to do the trick, 'what about me popping over there quickly by myself while you consolidate the main lines of the investigation at Frenchy Botham?' MacGregor was rather pleased with the way he had phrased that.

It worked like a dream.

'How long does it take to fly?' demanded Dover, capitulating to the green-eyed god of jealousy without a qualm.

16

A tactful veil will be drawn over the precise circumstances of
how they brought Dover to the Isle of Man. Suffice it to say that
Detective Sergeant MacGregor, British Airways, a *very* broad-
minded air hostess and a considerable amount of malt whisky
were all involved. It was agreed by those concerned that, such
was Dover's euphoria, he could probably have made the journey
without the assistance of powered flight, if pushed.

The Isle of Man police, whose co-operation had been requested
both as a matter of courtesy and in order to save time, had done
their job and the right Kincardine had been found without much
difficulty. This was the son of the Mrs Kincardine they had been
trying to trace, and an appointment was made for Dover and
MacGregor to see him. The Isle of Man police had also kindly
placed a car at the disposal of their distinguished visitors from
Scotland Yard.

The young police driver helped decant Dover into the back
seat. He was a fresh-faced, innocent lad who had come from a
rather sheltered home. His Inspector, who had heard about old
Wilf on the police grape-vine, had specially selected the boy for
the job, feeling that it would be a good idea to let him see something of the seamier side of life before the tourist season got into
full swing.

It was a comparatively short drive from the airport, which

was just as well as Dover wouldn't have the windows open and the young police driver was in grave danger of vicarious intoxication from the fumes.

Dover was in great form. Feeling happier now that he had got his bottom on terra firma, he gesticulated sketchily at the passersby. 'I thought everybody'd have three legs!' he quipped merrily. 'And the cats!' He turned to MacGregor. 'I thought all the bloody pussy cats'd have no tails and all the bloody people'd have three legs, eh?'

MacGregor pushed Dover back into his own corner and tried to make out that they weren't together.

Mr Kincardine turned out to be a man of noteworthy mediocrity. He ran a small ironmonger's shop and only managed to make ends meet by being amazingly unbusinesslike about Value Added Tax and other fiscal matters. He took Dover and MacGregor through to a back room while his wife took charge in the shop. She was congenitally incapable of adding two and two together but, since her mistakes were rarely in the customer's favour, Mr Kincardine didn't mind letting her stand in for him occasionally.

The back room was really more of a store room but it contained a couple of chairs and a table and Mr Kincardine thought it would do. MacGregor picked out the sturdier looking chair and dumped Dover on it before getting down to brass tacks.

'Oh, I expect it's her,' said Mr Kincardine obligingly. After all, they had come all the way from the mainland to see him.

MacGregor pushed the photograph of Pearl Wallace back into Mr Kincardine's clammy hands. 'Don't you know?'

Mr Kincardine was apologetic. 'These young ladies all look much of a muchness, don't they. Long hair and great green circles round their eyes.'

'Maybe,' said Dover, clawing his way up to the surface for a moment's unpleasantness, 'you were paying more attention to her figure than her face, you dirty devil!'

Mr Kincardine blenched. The shrewdness of the bleary-eyed fat man terrified him. God knows, there'd been enough trouble about that other girl without . . . He tried to smile at MacGregor. 'Yes, it's her, all right,' he said, 'Definitely.'

'And she came here to see you?'

'Yes.'

'When?'

'Oh, it's a couple of weeks ago, maybe three.' Mr Kincardine consulted a wall calendar which was covered with enigmatic signs. 'It'd be Tuesday the eleventh.' He pointed to a thick blue circle round the date. 'That's the day they deliver the paraffin. The tanker was just driving off when she arrived. She asked if she could have a few words with me so I invited her into the sitting room upstairs.'

Dover, who seemed to have sex on the brain, interrupted again. 'Upstairs, eh?'

'The smell of the paraffin,' explained Mr Kincardine with an ingratiating smile. 'This room was reeking with it. Otherwise I'd have talked to her in here, of course.'

Dover leered. 'Of course! Was your wife in?'

'Er, no, she was out.'

'Fancy!' sneered Dover, finding Mr Kincardine guilty as charged and with no extenuating circumstances. 'You do surprise me!'

'I kept the door open at the top of the stairs,' gabbled Mr Kincardine, anxious to demonstrate that all the proprieties had been observed. 'In case a customer came into the shop.'

But Dover was no longer listening, being once again obliged to lend an ear to the urgent promptings of one of his inner men. There was a message coming up that it would be injudicious to ignore. Dover broke into Mr Kincardine's feeble apologia. 'Where's your toilet?'

'Eh? Oh, upstairs!' Mr Kincardine pulled himself together. 'I'll show you.'

'Don't bother!' Dover much preferred exploring other people's houses in the absence of their owners. 'I'll find it.'

Mr Kincardine and MacGregor waited in respectful silence as Dover thumped his laborious way up the stairs to the living quarters above the shop. MacGregor, fastidiously anxious to hear no more, put the whole sordid little incident right behind him and went on with his questions.

'Did she tell you her name?'

Mr Kincardine thought, 'No, I don't think she did. She just said she was the representative of this organization that traces your family tree sort of thing, and could I give her some information about our family.'

'And you believed her?'

'Why not? I was a bit surprised, of course, because our family's nothing special. Ordinary working-class people on both sides, as far as I know. Mind you, the girl did strike me as a bit – well – unprepossessing. I've had a fair bit of experience over the years, what with salesmen and reps and what-have-you. There's a certain style about them. They want something out of you and they turn on the charm to get it. Now, this girl hadn't the faintest idea how to go about it. There she was, trying to get me to give her some information or whatever for free, and she didn't even look *clean*. And as for trying on a bit of the old sex appeal ... No, I should have been on my guard.'

'Did you give her the information she wanted?'

'Well, not exactly,' said Mr Kincardine. 'You see, she explained that her company or society or whatever-it-was was particularly interested in my mother's side of the family. In fact, what it all boiled down to was that, if I could put her in touch with my mother, she wouldn't need to trouble me at all. Well, that's when I had to tell her that my mother had passed away four years ago. And then she asked me if I knew anything about any nieces my mother had had – my cousins they would be, of course. She was especially interested in one called Jones – Muriel Jones.'

MacGregor felt a warm glow of satisfaction flood over him. At last – and in spite of Dover's best endeavours – they were beginning to get somewhere. Some pieces, at least, of the jig-saw puzzle were beginning to slot into place. 'Muriel Jones,' he echoed encouragingly. 'And have you got a cousin called Muriel Jones, Mr Kincardine?'

'No, not called Jones. I've got one called Muriel, of course.

She's the daughter of one of my mother's younger sisters. Mind you, I haven't laid eyes on her since we were kids, though I've got an idea my mother kept in touch with her a lot longer.'

'And you told the girl all this?'

'Yes, I did.'

'And what was her reaction?'

'Well, she seemed quite pleased. Excited, almost. She asked if she could have this cousin's address so that she could get in touch with her direct.'

'And you gave it to her?'

'No.' Mr Kincardine shook his head. 'Well, in any case, I haven't got her address but I was beginning to get a mite suspicious. I mean, it could have been for anything, couldn't it? Bad debts, tax evasion ...'

'So what did you do?'

'I told the girl I hadn't got my cousin's address, but that I thought I could get in touch with her. If she – that's the girl – would like to send me a proper letter from her firm, I'd do my best to get it forwarded to my cousin who could then reply or not as she wanted. That seemed to me the most satisfactory way of dealing with the problem.'

'Very business-like!' approved MacGregor. 'And the girl – Pearl Wallace – she was equally happy about the arrangements?'

Mr Kincardine grinned ruefully. 'Not exactly. She got a bit agitated and rather aggressive. She started spinning some fantastic yarn about this being her big chance to earn a fat commission from her firm and the client was a rich American who wanted quick results and they hadn't time to go through all this rigmarole and couldn't I just tell her where she could get in touch with my cousin, Muriel, even if I hadn't got the exact address.'

'And eventually you succumbed to her blandishments?' MacGregor had heard that some men were constitutionally incapable of refusing a young woman anything. Privately he fancied that he would have found Pearl Wallace highly resistible, but Mr Kincardine's tastes might be different.

'No, I didn't, as a matter of fact.' Mr Kincardine grinned and treated MacGregor to a sly, sideways glance. 'I won't say that we couldn't have reached some mutually satisfactory agreement, given time,' he admitted. 'What with the wife being out for the day and me not owing Cousin Muriel anything, when you came to think about it. The kid wasn't all that bad looking, and she was young. However' – Mr Kincardine sighed deeply – 'the best laid plans of rats and men ...'

'What happened?'

'The bloody shop bell went, didn't it,' said Mr Kincardine crossly. 'I had to go down. I get enough stock nicked when I'm standing there watching 'em without leaving the place unattended. I was probably away five minutes. When I got back, she'd scarpered. Vamoosed. Done a bunk.'

MacGregor stared hard at Mr Kincardine. 'Just like that?' he queried.

'Well, no,' said Mr Kincardine reluctantly, lowering his voice just in case his wife was behind the door listening, 'she took fifty quid with her.'

'Fifty quid?'

'From the cash box in my desk. I keep it up there for bloody safety,' he added bitterly.

MacGregor was mildly irritated. When he requested co-operation from the local police, he expected to get it. The Isle of Man coppers had found Mr Kincardine for him efficiently enough. Why hadn't they also briefed him about this theft? It had been very remiss of them, unless ...

Mr Kincardine, who had seated himself on a packing case, squirmed uneasily. 'No, I didn't report it to the police,' he whispered. 'I didn't want to get the girl into trouble, did I?'

MacGregor's elegant eyebrows shot up.

Mr Kincardine decided that honesty might well be his best policy. 'It was just a sort of little nest egg I was hiding from the Income Tax people,' he hissed. 'If I'd told the police about it, it might have led to more damned trouble than it was worth.' He managed a sickly smile. 'I mean, what's fifty quid these days? Chicken feed, eh?'

MacGregor was more concerned with the fate of Pearl Wallace

than with Mr Kincardine's financial shenanigans. 'And you've no idea why she left so abruptly?'

'I concluded that she'd got what she came for – the cash.'

'So all this stuff about tracing ancestors and your cousin's address – you think that was simply part of the con?'

Mr Kincardine shrugged his shoulders. 'It doesn't sound very likely, I'll admit. Too elaborate by half. But what other explanation is there? If she really wanted to get in touch with Muriel, she'd have stuck around until I got back, wouldn't she?'

'Unless she'd already found the information for herself,' said MacGregor, 'while you were in the shop. Well, she obviously went hunting around in your desk.'

'But, I told you,' protested Mr Kincardine, 'I haven't got Muriel's address!'

'There must be something,' said MacGregor.

'There isn't! Definitely not!' Mr Kincardine was adamant. Then his face changed. 'Unless ...'

Meanwhile Chief Inspector Dover had been answering a rather lengthy call of Nature up in the Kincardines' blue and gold bathroom. As befits the establishment of an ironmonger, the place was full of expensive accessories and gadgets, most of which were securely bolted to the wall. Dover absent-mindedly pocketed a piece of soap that seemed to be going spare and then went foraging around the rest of the flat.

The first room he came to was the lounge and, since it seemed quite a promising proposition, he went in, moving with remarkable stealth for a man of his age, weight and general clumsiness. It would, of course, be grossly unfair to suggest that Dover was going to *steal* anything. It was just that sometimes in his line of business, in the stress of the moment, people simply forgot to offer the usual hospitality. It slipped their minds. In such circumstances self-help was almost obligatory.

It didn't take a detective of Dover's calibre and experience long to find out that the Kincardines didn't smoke. Nor did the stingy devils keep a few for their friends. The biscuit barrel on the mantelpiece contained nothing more exciting than a couple

F

of cream crackers, both of which were soggy. Dover, disgruntled, moved across the room to have a look at the desk, and it was at this point that the photograph caught his eye. Well, not so much the photograph, perhaps, as the frame it was in. Which was silver and highly portable.

Highly, Dover corrected himself as he picked it up for a closer look, pocketable, actually. He wondered, idly, what such a small, silver frame would fetch these days on the open market. Not enough, he concluded sadly, to make it worth his while risking his pension. He was putting the photograph back on the top of the desk when he belatedly realized just what it was he was looking at. It was the rather stiffly posed picture of a young woman. The hair style was different, the make-up looked old fashioned and the marks of some twenty years of living were missing from the face, but Dover knew who it was. By God, he did! He'd seen that face within the last few days. So recently, in fact, that he hadn't had time to forget it. That – he would stake his life on it – was What's-her-name!

In an absolute tizzy of exaltation and excitement, Dover read the inscription. It was scrawled in a bold hand across the bottom corner of the photograph: *To dear Aunty Flo, with much love, Muriel.*

Dover tossed the photograph back on the desk and went hurtling down the stairs with all the dignity and restraint of a bull elephant in rut. He burst into the little back room where the interview between MacGregor and the mildly dishonest, mildly libidinous Mr Kincardine was about to reach its climax.

Inspiration and sudden recollection had, as careful readers will remember, just struck Mr Kincardine. He had realized that there *was* something upstairs in his lounge which was connected with his cousin Muriel and which the dead girl might have seen. He was about to reveal all to MacGregor when Dover arrived.

'Come on!' roared Dover, in such a bustle that he didn't even bother to sit down.

MacGregor scrambled to his feet, the chill hand of apprehension already clutching at his heart. 'Come on where, sir?' he enquired.

Dover was already on his way. 'Back to civilization, laddie!' he bawled over his shoulder. 'I've solved the case! No point in mucking around this dump any longer.'

MacGregor felt everything begin to go black before his eyes. The shock of having his worst fears fulfilled was almost too much for him. Could that old fool, Dover, really have solved the case? MacGregor would have rather had a dozen murderers walk away scot free than ... No! MacGregor pulled himself together. He mustn't even allow himself to think such subversive thoughts.

Pausing only to snatch up his notebook, MacGregor chased through one of the most interesting selections of ironmongery in the Isle of Man and was just in time to see Dover clambering into the waiting police car. There had actually been a slight delay as the young police driver was unaware that Dover didn't open doors for himself if there was some underling there to do it for him. The young police driver knew better now, of course.

'Sir!' MacGregor shoved the driver aside before he could shut the door. 'We can't leave now, sir! I haven't finished questioning Mr Kincardine.'

'Tough,' said Dover who watched an awful lot of American cops-and-robbers on the telly.

'You don't understand, sir.' MacGregor made a conscious effort not to sink begging to his knees. 'While she was here, Pearl Wallace must have found some clue to her mother's whereabouts. That's why she left without waiting for Mr Kincardine to come back.'

Dover grinned like a particularly nasty-minded Cheshire Cat.

MacGregor swallowed his tears of frustration. 'Mr Kincardine was just about to tell me what it was, sir.'

'You don't say!' said Dover, still grinning.

'Just five minutes, sir! Please!'

Dover settled himself well back. 'Get in, laddie!' he said. 'This case is all over bar the shouting.'

MacGregor glanced at his watch. 'We've got at least a couple of hours before the plane leaves, sir. Surely we ...'

Dover's beady little button eyes peered spitefully out from

under the brim of his bowler hat. 'They've got a bar at the bloody airport, haven't they?'

MacGregor made one last effort. 'Suppose I hang on here for a few more minutes, sir – just to get a proper signed statement from Mr Kincardine and tie up a few loose ends? Then I could get a taxi and join you later at the airport.'

Dover's glance was almost pitying. MacGregor must be going bloody soft in the head if he thought a trick like that was going to work. 'Get in, laddie!' he grunted again. 'There's a hell of a draught with that door open.'

17

Now that he was in position to place his grubby hand on the shrinking shoulder of the murderer of Pearl Wallace, Dover had every intention of making a full-scale spectacular out of it. It so rarely happened that he brought a case to a successful conclusion that he was determined everybody should know about it when he did. He wanted the full VIP treatment waiting for him at Frenchy Botham – red carpet, TV cameras, brass band, civic welcome and a motor cycle escort. It was MacGregor's unenviable task to organize this august reception, working from a public telephone in Ronaldsway Airport while Dover held court in the cocktail lounge.

Wearily MacGregor picked his way through the crowd of admirers and interrupted some yarn about how Dover (single-handed) had arrested a champion middle-weight wrestler who was running amuck in a Soho vice den with a meat cleaver. 'I'm afraid it's as I expected, sir,' he said, wasting his irony on the smoke and whisky-ladened air. 'The magistrates won't issue a warrant without the name of the person involved. Of course, sir, if you could just tell me who it is, we could have the warrant all ready and waiting.'

Dover's wits hadn't been dulled that much by free drink. 'You've got What's-his-name standing by, though?'

MacGregor nodded. 'Inspector Walters will be there, sir. I've just been speaking to him personally.' MacGregor tried to get some consolation from the knowledge that he'd finally got it into Dover's thick skull that the actual arrest had to be made by a member of the local police force. Dover didn't seem to be aware of this and had been looking forward to slipping on the handcuffs, himself. He had not taken it well when he had been told that this moment of glory would belong to Inspector Walters. 'And I've laid on supper at The Laughing Dog, sir, for after the arrest.'

Dover took that in all right. '*After?*'

'There's a dining car on the train, sir. I thought we could have something to eat on the way down and then ...'

'Yes, yes! All right!' Dover was anxious to get back to his open-handed chums and finish off his tale of valour, derring-do and fiction. 'That it?'

MacGregor consulted his list. 'Car at Chapminster ... local TV people warned ... local newspaper people warned ...' He looked up. 'There is just one thing, sir. It's going to be rather late by the time we get to Frenchy Botham. Wouldn't it be better to postpone the whole thing till tomorrow morning? We could keep the suspect under surveillance and ...'

'Get lost, laddie!' said Dover, and returned to pinning back a few more credulous ears.

It was indeed rather late before British Rail disgorged Dover and MacGregor back to Chapminster. Inspector Walters was patiently waiting for them with a car. He had been rather taken aback to find that 'his' murder had been solved, apparently on the Isle of Man, but he had decided not to raise his Chief Constable's hopes until they'd got the whole thing cut and dried. Somehow Inspector Walters couldn't quite rid himself of the notion that Chief Inspector Dover really was the fat, stupid, lazy slob he looked. This made it difficult to believe that he could do anything properly and Inspector Walters, rather foolishly, preferred not to involve his superior officer until he was quite sure.

If Inspector Walters had been looking forward to some sort of comradely reunion, he was sadly disappointed. Both the Scotland Yard men were weary and travel stained, and one of them was apparently still suffering from train sickness. When Dover eventually emerged from the gents' lavatory on Chapminster station the police car set off for Frenchy Botham.

At first the atmosphere was one of expectant silence. Then Inspector Walters was obliged to ask the question. 'Where to in Frenchy Botham, sir?'

'The Grove,' grunted Dover.

'Any particular house, sir?' Inspector Walters fished with more hope than MacGregor had done, but with an equal lack of success.

'Nope,' said Dover who was determined to stretch out his moment of glory as long as possible. 'Tell the driver to stop at the top and we'll walk from there.'

And walk they did, their footsteps lit by the light of an evasive moon and the stronger beam of Inspector Walters's electric torch.

'That's Lilac View, sir,' said Inspector Walters, illuminating a gatepost and a short stretch of gravelled drive. 'Mr de la Poche. I suppose we're hardly likely to be calling there looking for the mother of the Wallace girl – not with him being a bachelor and everything.'

'You never know these days,' growled Dover, his feet making him disinclined for conversation. 'Who lives in this one?'

'This is Fairacre, sir.' Inspector Walters played his torch on a clump of hydrangeas and the little cortege veered slightly in this new direction. 'That's the bank manager, sir. Mr Talbot. He and his wife are the ones who dabble in all this spirit nonsense. Could Mrs Talbot be the one you're after?'

Inspector Walters paused interrogatively, but Dover plodded painfully on.

Remembering the incident of What Had Happened to the Bowler Hat, Inspector Walters left it to MacGregor to do the honours at the next house. After all, the Sergeant knew as much about the inhabitants of The Grove as anybody did. MacGregor duly poked Dover's failing memory into life with the utmost care. 'Otterly House, sir. That's the youngish couple – Peter and

Maddie Bones – with the French au pair girl and the three small – er – children, if you remember.'

' I remember all bloody right,' muttered Dover darkly. ' Mucky little bugger!'

'The Bones's are the ones, sir, who had his boss and wife to dinner and ...'

' Where's the telly?' demanded Dover suddenly. ' And the newspaper men?' He swung round on Inspector Walters. ' I thought you were supposed to be laying a bit of publicity on?'

Inspector Walters backed off, in order to protect the innocent. 'Sergeant MacGregor did ask me, sir, but I'm afraid it's against our Standing Orders. I did check. The Chief Constable apparently likes investigations and particularly arrests to be carried out with as much discretion as possible. He thinks it's only fair for the protection of the person or persons involved.'

' 'Strewth!' said Dover in tones of the deepest disgust. ' A fine bloody pal you've turned out to be! You could have tipped 'em off on the bloody quiet, couldn't you? God damn it, I'd have done it myself if I'd known you were going to be so bloody weak-kneed about it. Where the hell's this?'

Confused by the abrupt change of subject, Inspector Walters let his torch waver. Then he got his bearings. 'Ah, this is Ilfracombe, sir. Where Mrs Esmond Gough lives with her retired brigadier husband. She's the founder of the Sorority for Sacerdotal Sex Equality, as I expect you remember. She wants women to have the right to be ordained as priests.'

' She wants her bloody head examining!' grunted Dover. ' Silly cow!'

MacGregor, stumbling along in the dark behind old Master Mind, tried frantically to work it out. There was only Miss Charlotte Henty-Harris left! But, surely, she was far too old to be Pearl Wallace's mother? No doubt it was biologically possible – MacGregor did some rapid mental arithmetic – yes, just. But everybody had talked of the mysterious Miss Jones as a young woman. Even eighteen years ago Miss Henty-Harris would have been well into her forties. The sweat began to run down Mac-Gregor's back. Could it be that the mysterious Miss Jones was only a decoy? A stand-in? Could Pearl Wallace's mother actually be somebody quite different? If so, though, how the hell had Dover ever unravelled the complications?

'Oh, sorry, sir!' MacGregor bumped into Dover who had stopped dead in his tracks to listen to Inspector Walters's final oration.

'Watch it!' squealed Dover, viewing as always any physical contact with MacGregor with the utmost suspicion. 'You keep your hands to yourself, laddie!'

The darkness mercifully spared MacGregor's blushes.

'And that was where Miss Henty-Harris found the body, sir,' concluded Inspector Walters lamely. He shone his torch on the fatal shrubbery behind the open gate. Inspector Walters didn't know what the hell was going on between these two Scotland Yard men, but, in his opinion, the sooner the pair of them cleared off back to London, the better for all concerned. 'Shall we go in, sir? There's a light on in the front room so it looks as though Miss Henty-Harris is still up.'

'Go in?' In the light of the torch Dover's pasty face looked even more oafish than usual. 'What the hell for?'

'Er – aren't you going to charge Miss Henty-Harris with the murder, sir?'

'You taken leave of your senses or something?' enquired Dover with insulting mock concern. 'It's not her I'm after, you blockhead, it's the other one!'

'Sir?'

'What's-her-name!' explained Dover with mounting exasperation. 'That silly cow who wants to go poncing around in a dog-collar!'

'Mrs Esmond Gough, sir?' It was MacGregor who found his voice first. 'She murdered Pearl Wallace? Are you sure?'

'Of course I'm bloody sure!' snapped Dover. 'Come on, get a bloody move on! We don't want to be taking all night about it. I haven't had my bloody supper yet.' And, so saying, he marched off firmly and resolutely in the wrong direction.

The confrontation between Mrs Esmond Gough and Dover

was something of a disappointment all round. Mrs Esmond Gough was obviously disconcerted to find that the connection between her and the dead girl had been traced by a mere male, while Dover, who not only didn't mind but actually preferred thumping the truth out of weak and helpless females, was profoundly frustrated when his intended victim didn't put up a fight. Brigadier Gough appeared to have been struck dumb and Inspector Walters wondered exhaustedly why the hell it all had to take so long.

Sergeant MacGregor was the worst sufferer, of course, and it took all his training and sense of discipline not to give way to a temper tantrum when it quickly became established that Dover, by whatever quirk of Fate, had indeed hit the jackpot. His opening statement – made from a deep armchair and with his feet stretched out towards the Goughs' sitting room fire – had blown the lid clean off.

'I've just come from the Isle of Man,' was all Dover had said, or needed to say.

Mrs Esmond Gough's noble face had turned to stone. 'That,' she commented bitterly to the room at large, ' is what one gets for giving way to one's better feelings. Damn!' She looked angrily at Dover. ' It was that photograph, wasn't it?'

Dover nodded, and MacGregor wondered if he dared ask what photograph they were talking about. After all, it was his job to record the interview and if he didn't know what they were talking ...

'I thought so,' said Mrs Esmond Gough, giving a tight, affirmative toss of her head. 'Good old Auntie Flo! I should never have been such a fool as to have sent it to her in the first place, but she'd been so kind to me and I knew she'd keep my secret to the grave.'

'The secret that you'd given birth to an illegitimate child?' asked MacGregor, risking Dover's wrath in an effort to make sure that he had got the facts right.

'Of course.' Mrs Esmond Gough glanced at MacGregor as though he'd just crawled out from under an exceptionally slimy stone. 'Oh, I know it's not supposed to matter two hoots these days, but twenty years ago it was a very different story. Especially for somebody of my age and standing. I was twenty-six, you know, and a university graduate. Not the type of girl to whom such "mistakes" are easily forgiven. My father had married beneath him, you know, with the result that my mother was socially and financially a great deal better off than the remainder of her family. She never actually lost touch with them, but contact did tend to be rather spasmodic. When I found out I was pregnant the only thing to do was to go and hide myself away somewhere, have the child and then get it adopted. I didn't fancy having a back street abortion and, in any case, I hadn't the least idea how to go about getting one. Auntie Flo was wonderful. She sheltered me, made all the arrangements for everything – and I knew I could rely on her to keep her mouth shut. She even went along with the fact that I was using an assumed name. On reflection I think I might have picked something a little more imaginative than Jones, but it seemed nice and anonymous at the time.'

MacGregor couldn't really believe that Dover had dozed off there in his comfy chair, but his eyes were closed and his breathing was suspiciously regular. 'You were lying then when you told us that you were unable to have children?'

'Naturally,' said Mrs Esmond Gough indifferently. 'I was trying to put you off the scent.'

'And the child you gave birth to was Pearl Wallace, the dead girl?'

'Presumably.' Mrs Esmond Gough seemed to resent these questions much as she would have resented impertinence in a servant. 'I certainly had a female child. Miss Wallace herself had no doubt that I was her mother.'

'She called here to see you that Wednesday evening?'

Mrs Esmond Gough nodded. 'She came round to the back door. She was that sort of person. I was, as I told you, in the kitchen painting the posters for our Rally.'

'You asked her in?'

'Of course. I didn't have much choice. It was a simply filthy night and, anyhow, I assumed she was one of our helpers or a new recruit or something. She'd traced me through that photograph, you know. The one I'd sent Auntie Flo when I first started making a name for myself with my work. Who'd have thought the dear old thing would have kept it all these years – or that that dratted son of hers wouldn't have thrown it away when she died.'

Dover stirred gently in his chair. 'You're the family celebrity,' he pointed out sleepily. 'A household name. I reckon that's why he hung onto it. Besides,' he added through one of his jaw-unhinging yawns, 'it was in a silver frame.'

'If I hadn't been a household name,' Mrs Esmond Gough commented tartly, 'that girl would never have found me – and neither would you! She recognized me, you see, even though that photograph was taken donkey's years ago. She knew her mother's Christian name was Muriel – they'd told her that at the adoption society or wherever – and once she'd read my signature the rest was too easy. She'd tied her mother up to Mrs Esmond Gough.'

'How did she know where to find you?' asked MacGregor curiously. 'She seems to have come straight here from the Isle of Man.'

'There'd been a magazine article about me in *Buttons & Beaux*. That's one of these dreadful teenager magazines – terrible rubbish, but they pay quite incredibly well. Unfortunately they happened to mention that I lived near Chapminster. God knows why a ridiculous fact like that stuck in the girl's head, but it did. Just my luck! Once she got as far as Chapminster it wasn't, I imagine, difficult to discover my address.'

'She looked it up in the phone book,' said MacGregor. He turned over to a clean page in his notebook. 'Did she say why she'd gone to all this trouble to seek you out?'

Mrs Esmond Gough's eyebrows rose indignantly. 'She wanted money! She was threatening to blackmail me! It was absolutely outrageous! It would have been bad enough if she'd come searching for me out of affection but – for hard cash? *That* was unforgivable!'

'Did she say how much she wanted?' asked MacGregor,

fancying he saw Mrs Esmond Gough, who was nobody's fool, beginning to lay down the lines of her defence. English juries are notorious for disliking blackmailers.

'I didn't give her the chance!' Mrs Esmond Gough drew herself up proudly. 'I listened patiently to all this stuff about what a rotten life she'd had with her adopted parents and how she'd never had a chance and how she'd got herself pregnant and that it was all my fault for rejecting her in the first place. Well, I listened to all that but, when she started talking about how much the newspapers would pay for her story, I'm afraid I completely lost my temper.'

'And killed her?'

Mrs Esmond Gough wasn't listening. 'The little bitch was out to ruin me! Oh, the church is very progressive and broad-minded nowadays but you can be quite certain about one thing – the first woman to be ordained in the Church of England will not be the mother of an illegitimate child. I could see all my work going for nothing. Those years and years of meetings and demonstrations and interviews and protests. All the travelling. All the organizing. All the pushing and the cajoling and the bullying and bribing. The endless sneers and the continued insults!' She sucked in a deep, almost sobbing breath. 'Well, no stupid, interfering, insolent chit of a girl was going to take all that away from me!'

'But I thought you were accusing her of blackmail?' Inspector Walters wasn't used to playing third fiddle on occasions like this and he had a few questions of his own to ask. 'She was threatening to expose you if you didn't pay her money – right? Well, madam, you had the remedy in your own hands. All you had to do was come along to us. We would have protected you – and preserved your anonymity into the bargain.'

Mrs Esmond Gough stared coldly at Inspector Walters. 'I don't, my good man,' she said as she squashed him right out of the proceedings, 'have any anonymity! My name is a household word and my face is known from one end of the country to the other. That's why the solution you are suggesting of going to the police was completely out of the question. I am just too famous.

Besides, whatever I had done about the blackmail threats, even submitting to them, would have been to no avail. That girl would have betrayed me. I could see it in her face. No power on earth would have stopped her.'

MacGregor sighed. He got a little tired from time to time with murderers who insisted that they'd had no other choice.

Mrs Esmond Gough declaimed on, looking and sounding like a tragedy queen. 'It was revenge she wanted. Revenge on me, on her boyfriend, on society, on the world!' The mask slipped a little. 'That little bitch was just itching to expose me. Besides, where was I to get the money from? I'm not a wealthy woman. All I earn is ploughed straight back into the Cause.'

Dover was getting hungry. Dinner on the train might have been wildly expensive but it wasn't filling. His stomach, longing for the super-stodge served up at The Laughing Dog, started rumbling quite loudly. 'So,' he said, hoping to speed things up, 'you croaked her, eh?'

Mrs Esmond Gough drew herself up. Those fine eyes flashed and that noble bosom heaved. 'I certainly did not!' she retorted indignantly. 'Such a course of action would be not only against my most cherished beliefs, but against all my instincts as well. The girl was my own flesh and blood, after all. No, as soon as I realized precisely what she was up to, I fetched my husband. And he killed her. I'm sorry, Esmond' – she turned to address the Brigadier who seemed to be in considerable doubt as to what had hit him – 'but we have always agreed that my vocation must come first. With the March of Religious Women next Tuesday and the burning of the Pope in effigy on Saturday, I really can't afford to be shut up in prison on remand. If there was any question of my getting bail, it would be a different matter, of course, but they don't give bail if one is on a charge of murder. In any case, dear' – she smiled encouragingly at him – 'the truth is bound to come out in the end and it's really much more convenient to reveal your part in the incident at this stage rather than wait for the actual trial. That mightn't take place for months, you know.'

MacGregor had been attempting to interrupt for some time.

Dear heavens, there were cautions and all sorts of routine things to carry out.

Mrs Esmond Gough's flow was not, however, to be stemmed. Well, not by a mere sergeant, at any rate. She held up her hand to silence him and launched herself into a brisk exposition of the murder as she saw it. 'My husband came into the kitchen at my request and I explained our predicament to him. He attempted to remonstrate with the girl but her response to his overtures was extremely rude and insolent. Thus provoked, Esmond seized the nearest heavy implement – an electric iron, as it happens – and struck the girl several violent blows on the head. No, no, my dear' – the Brigadier seemed anxious to make some statement on his own behalf – 'it's much better that you shouldn't say anything at this stage. Wait until we can get you a solicitor. Now, do be guided by me, my dear! You know that I've had considerably more experience of criminal proceedings than you have. Now, where was I? Oh yes, well, when we realized that the girl was dead, my husband got his wheelbarrow from the garden shed and took the body away to dispose of it. While he was attending to this, I cleaned up the kitchen – thanking my lucky stars, I don't mind telling you, that I'd had the floor tiled last year. I can really recommend it. One wipe with a damp cloth and it all comes up as good as new. Oh, and I burnt the girl's handbag in the boiler. Without examining the contents, of course. I may have my faults, but vulgar curiosity is not one of them. Well, now' – Mrs Esmond Gough rose gracefully to her feet – 'I think that about covers everything. I would appreciate it if we could get the preliminaries over as expeditiously as possible. I've got an especially heavy day tomorrow. I have to go up to London to see the printers and then I'm preaching in the evening in Wapping.' She smiled round at her audience as, with the notable exception of Dover, they began standing up in their turn. 'By the way, do any of you gentlemen have any contacts at Scotland Yard with whoever it is who deals with processions and marches?'

Dover and MacGregor followed the Esmond Goughs out of the

house to where a couple of police cars were waiting to drive them away. Husband and wife were to travel separately and Mrs Esmond Gough was already chatting earnestly away to the stolid policewoman who was her escort.

Dover picked his way gingerly down the front steps. 'She's going to get one hell of a shock when she finds they're going to keep her in the nick.'

MacGregor agreed. 'I don't think it's registered with her yet that she's going to be charged as an accessory to murder. I suppose, sir' – he helped Dover negotiate the last two steps – 'you saw this photograph in Mr Kincardine's sitting room?'

'That's right!' Dover grabbed hold of MacGregor's arm and clung on tightly as they made their way down the drive which seemed very dark now that the police cars with their headlights had purred softly away. 'That woman's got a very distinctive face, you know. Twenty years hasn't made all that much difference. I knew as soon as I saw that snap that I'd got the murderer.'

'Well' – MacGregor couldn't, in the interests of accuracy, let that remark pass – 'it would appear that Brigadier Gough is the actual killer.'

Dover was in a benign mood. 'I said it was him all along, didn't I?' he asked happily. 'Right at the bloody beginning I said he was our man.' He smiled complacently in the darkness as he hobbled along. 'Even if I says it as shouldn't, laddie, I do have a nose for these things!'